THE RANGER'S CHOICE

A NOVEL BY
CONNIE CARSON

Publisher's Cataloging-in-Publication Data
1. Cowboy—Fiction 2. Texas History—Fiction 3. Texas Rangers—Fiction
PS 3356C319 2014   Fic Car
ISBN 978-009906120-2-5
Library of Congress Control Nu

Dedicated to the memory of
Betty Snyder
and
T. P. Jones, Texas Ranger

A special thank you to Betty Snyder and Sandra Jeschke for
allowing me to use their names in this book.

Other Works of Fiction by Connie Carson

Colonial Romance

The Bugle's Call

Texas Bound

The Marshal's Lady

The Cowboy's Cousin

Chapter 1

Apache Flats, Texas 1876

"Hey, handsome!" the woman called out, as Diego walked quickly past her. "Whatcha' in such a hurry about? Out here nobody hurries nowhere."

"I'm a newcomer to these parts. I guess I haven't learned that yet," Diego answered, with a smile.

"My name's Lapopa."

"I'm Diego Black."

"Well, Diego Black, come on in the cantina an' let me buy ya' something to cool ya' off. I think we could be real good friends in jest a bit," she said, smiling seductively at him.

"Ma'am, I think I had best let you know, right now, I'm a married man and I have no intention of getting familiar with you or any woman besides my wife." He said this as he looked at her tight fitting, low cut bodice of her dress.

"Where's yer wife at?" Lapopa asked.

"Bexar County."

"That's a long ways from here. She won't never know," Lapopa cooed. She took his arm and attempted to lead him into the cantina.

"Lady, I've tried to be nice, but the answer to your proposition is No! and it will always be No! You might as well get that straight right now," he said in a firm voice as pulled his arm away.

"What's wrong with ya'? No man ever turns Lapopa down! Are ya' ascared of yer wife?" she sneered. "I didn't know the Texas Rangers hired yeller-bellied cowards," she added, as she jabbed her finger at his badge.

"You can think or say what you will, but you're not getting me to change my mind," Diego said, as he again removed her hand from his arm and proceeded down the street.

"We'll just see about that," Lapopa called out after him.

"I never thought I would see that happen," he heard a voice behind him say. "It's good to know there is somebody who can say no to Lapopa. I know I sure cain't. *Hola*! I'm Rafael Valverde."

"Glad to meet you, Rafael. I'm Diego Black." He turned toward the man and they shook hands. "I'm a newcomer to Apache Flats. Are all the women here as forward as Lapopa?"

"Only to handsome *gringos*." He laughed and then continued, "Let me warn ya', always keep a watch on yer back. Lots of 'em 'round here ain't fond of Texas Rangers." He pointed to the badge pinned to Diego's shirt. "The *senoritas* all carry knives and are as jest as handy with 'em as the men are with their guns, an' jest as eager to use 'em."

"Thanks for the warning."

"I heard they was sending a new Ranger out this way. Is Apache Flats gonna' be yer headquarters?"

"Yes. I just got here, this morning. My wife and sons will be coming in a couple of weeks or whenever I find a house for us to live in. I've been looking but I haven't had any luck. Do you have any ideas where I might find something?"

"Where ya' stayin' at now?" Rafael asked.

"In a room above the General Store."

"I been in that room. I know yer gonna be glad to get out of them cramped quarters as soon as ya' can. Are ya' willin' to offer a fair price fer a house?"

When Diego told him what he was willing to pay, Rafael smiled and said, "That's more 'an fair. Follow me, *mi amigo*, an' I will show ya' a house ya' can buy I think even yer wife will be pleased with."

They walked down the street until they came to a large frame house, one of the few frame houses Diego had seen since he'd arrived. With trees scarce in the area, lumber had to be brought in from several hundred miles away and was expensive. Because of that, most of the houses were adobe.

Rafael knocked on the door and, shortly, a middle-aged man answered. After he introduced the man to Diego, the two began speaking in rapid Spanish.

Diego tried to follow what they were saying but was only able to catch about half of what was being said. *I've noticed the majority of the people here are either Mexican or Indian,* he thought. *I don't know any Apache. I am fairly fluent in Spanish, it looks like I'm going to need to brush up on the language if I'm going to be living here. Since Vivienne's part Apache I know she knows a little of the language. Maybe she can teach me what she knows.*

After a few minutes the man looked at Diego and nodded his head.

"Ya' can bring the money to him tomorrow an' move in the next day," Rafael told Diego after they had thanked the man and were walking away from the house.

"How can that be? I didn't catch all of what you were saying, but I know you only offered him half of what I told you I was willing to pay."

"It is what I believe you *gringos* call blackmail. I know something 'bout the man's sister he don't want nobody to find out 'bout. I wouldn't mind if ya' shared a bit of that money I just saved ya'," he said with a sly grin.

"And if I say no?" Diego asked, returning the grin.

"Then somehow word will git to yer wife ya' slept with Lapopa before she got here." Rafael smiled.

"You drive a tough bargain." Diego laughed. "Is the information you have on the man's sister true or is it the work of your imagination?"

"I'll let ya' figure that out fer yerself," Rafael answered with a smile.

"Although yer paying much less fer the house than ya' told me ya' was willin' to spend, it was still a fair price. 'Specially since they been wantin' to sell it fer a long time now."

"Where are they going to find a place to live in such a short time?" Diego asked.

"Tha' house is much too big fer him an' his wife now all their *hijos* have left home. I happen to know their daughter has been wantin' them ta' move in with her an' her family. Believe me, they will enjoy spending yer money more than they would living in the house.

"*Senor* Rojas said they will be leavin' behind some furniture and other things they won't be needin' after they move in with their daughter."

"Good. Vivienne will be happy about that since we won't have any furniture until she gets here and orders what she wants."

"Ya' might give *Senor* Rojas a little extra *dinero* for what he is leaving."

"I'll bring some extra when I bring the money for the house tomorrow," Diego told him.

"Now, how about buyin' yer *nuevo amigo* a drink?"

"I was on my way back to the General Store to get some groceries, but your idea sounds much better. However, I'm not sure I'm ready just yet to face Lapopa again."

"Do not worry, *mi nuevo amigo*. Thar ain't much in Apache Flats, but we do have *tres cantinas*. I'm gonna' take ya' to one that is much better than where Lapopa works. The whiskey costs a little more but it goes down so much easier. And I know *mi nuevo rico amigo* can afford it," he said with a grin.

"In that case, *mi nuevo amigo*, let's go."

Diego had just moved into the house two days earlier and was trying to decide what to fix for lunch when there was a knock at the door. Upon answering it, a man who looked to be in his late forties and wearing a Texas Ranger badge was standing there.

"Howdy," the man said. "I'm Captain T. P. Jones. I'm assuming, since you're wearing a Ranger badge, you're

Lieutenant Diego Black."

"Yes sir, I am."

"Good. The reason you're home in the middle of the day had best be because you got my telegraph that I would be here today. Not because you're slacking on the job."

"Yes sir, I got your telegraph. I'm ready to start riding whenever you are."

"I've been in the saddle for a week. Nothing would please me more than to sit on something a little softer than a saddle and that doesn't move. Do you have an extra bed in here?"

"Yes sir. As a matter of fact, I do."

"Good. A nice soft, clean bed beats the hell out of a bedroll on the ground. We can get acquainted here just as well as we can out there in the dust and sun. Tomorrow will be soon enough to start our ride across your territory." The captain let out a deep sigh as he took off his hat and sat down in the one large overstuffed chair in the room. "I haven't been out this way in a while."

"I haven't had a chance to ride very far into the south part of the territory myself," Diego told him.

"In that case, that's where we'll head in the morning."

"Have you eaten?" Diego asked the captain.

"Are you cooking?" he asked.

"I am, if you're in a daring mood," Diego said.

"Right now, anything will be better than the hardtack and jerky I've been chewing on the past couple of days."

"You may change your mind about that after you've tasted my cooking," Diego told him.

"Tell me a little about yourself," the captain said after they had finished eating and were going into the sitting room. "I like to know something about the men I ride with."

"You probably know I'm married and have two sons. My family has a large cattle ranch in Bexar County near San Antonio and my father-in-law is the marshal in the small town near the ranch."

"How old are your sons?" the captain asked.

"Travis is seven and Charlie Joe is almost six."

"What made you decide your wanted to be a Ranger?"

"My family had a friend who was a Texas Ranger. He use to come to our ranch and visit with us when he was in the area. When he decided to retire from the Rangers my parents built him a house on the ranch where he lived until he died.

"He was the one who presented me with my badge at the swearing in ceremony. Just a few minutes after he gave me the badge he had a heart attack. He said he didn't want to die in a strange building in the middle of San Antonio. So we got a wagon and put him in it and raced back to the ranch. His last words to me that afternoon before he died were, 'Make the Rangers proud of you.' I've been trying to do that and to make him proud of me as well."

"What was his name? I might have known him."

"Joseph Travis."

"You have some big boots to fill."

"Then you did know him."

"I never met him, but I sure heard some might good things about him. He made quite a name for himself while he wore the Texas Ranger badge."

"So I'm finding out. I've yet to meet a Ranger who didn't either know him or know about him."

"What's this?" Diego asked a couple of days later when they rode up to some weather beaten houses and stores, all of which appeared to be empty.

"This is Flat Rock, Texas, or maybe I should say it was. It was deserted about five years ago when all the underground wells dried up."

"In other words, a ghost town," Diego said thoughtfully. "My sons would love this."

"How old did you say are they?"

"Seven and almost six."

"From the look on your face, I think you might enjoy it as much as they would."

"My wife has often accused me of not being any older than they are in a lot of ways," Diego said, returning the captain's smile.

"While we have the time, we might as well check things out here."

"Are you sure you want to do that?" Diego asked.

"I like to check out ghost towns as much as any man," the captain said with a smile.

They found a post to tie their horses to, dismounted, and started walking down the street, avoiding the decaying wooden sidewalk that ran in front of the stores.

"I've been through here several times and I've never seen a ghost, but I have seen numerous rattlesnakes. So, watch where you put your feet." They walked a little farther.

"Why the puzzled look on your face?" the captain asked when Diego suddenly stopped and tilted his head to one side.

"You said the town is deserted but I swear I hear music."

"The ghost of Flat Rock must like you. People usually don't hear that the first time they come here."

"Then I'm not imagining it?"

"Nope."

"Do you hear it?"

"No. But I have heard it several times in the past.

"Lack of water's not the only thing that caused the people here to leave. Shortly before everyone left, there was a gun-fight in the saloon where the music's coming from. Four men were killed. One of them was the man who played the piano in the saloon. A few days after the shooting, people began hearing the music. They believed it's the ghost of the piano player who's making the music."

"There's not even a piano in here," Diego said as he looked through the broken swinging doors into the saloon. "Now I know why you wanted to check out this ghost town. You wanted to see if I'd hear the music."

The captain just smiled.

"I think it's time we got back on the trail and start checking on the people who are of flesh and blood," Diego said, as he felt a cold shiver run down his spine. He turned away from the saloon and walked quickly toward his horse, unhitched it and mounted.

"It does get to you the first time you hear the music," the captain said, as they rode out of the town.

"I'm going to have to figure a way to get the boys here," Diego said thoughtfully, knowing Vivienne would be thoroughly opposed to the idea.

CHAPTER 2

The stage had stopped at a relay station to change horses and to let the passengers stretch their legs. Vivienne was talking to one of the other passengers and had her back to the door when she first heard Travis, then Charlie Joe yell, "Papa! Papa!"

Turning in disbelief, she saw Diego standing there, with a son in each arm, smiling at her. She rushed over to him and threw her arms around him. "I've missed you," she said with tears in her eyes.

"I've missed you too. Okay, boys. It's time for me to greet your mother properly," Diego said, as he put them down.

"Diego, there are people watching," she said quietly.

"Yes, there are," he said. He looked around the room full of people, who had all turned in their direction and were watching them.

"Folks, I haven't seen my wife in over a month. I'm sure you wouldn't mind if I kissed her, would you?" His words caused laughter to burst through the room.

"You enjoy embarrassing me, don't you?" Vivienne asked.

"Yes. You're beautiful when you blush," he said, as he watched her blush deepen. "Now, I'm going to get that kiss." With that he lowered his head and gave her a long awaited kiss as everyone cheered.

"What are you doing here?" Vivienne asked when their lips parted.

"Well, this area is in my territory so I decided to patrol

around here so I could see you a day early.

"If I don't want the stagecoach to leave without me I'd better go buy a ticket," he said, as he took Vivienne's hand and they walked toward the counter.

"I don't know whether there will be room for you on the stagecoach. It's already full," Vivienne told him.

"Sir, you're more than welcome to have my seat. I'll be glad to sit on top," one of the passengers said, as he walked over to where Diego and Vivienne were standing.

"Are you sure you want to do that?" Vivienne asked.

"Yes, ma'am. It'll be my pleasure to do something for the Texas Rangers. I've got a ranch south of here and the Rangers have helped me with problems more than once. It's the least I can do."

"Thank you," Diego said. "My family and I appreciate your kind offer."

"See, our kiss paid off," Diego whispered in Vivienne's ear, as they walked to the desk to buy his ticket.

He tied his horse to the back of the coach, and was helping Vivienne inside when Travis said, "Papa, can I sit on your lap?"

"Me too!" Charlie Joe exclaimed.

"Well, let's see," he said thoughtfully. "There are two of you and I have two knees, so I guess that can be done."

After a hot dusty ride and a night spent at another relay station, they arrived in Apache Flats. "Oh my! This is a very small town," Vivienne said the next day when she stepped off the coach and looked around the town she would now be calling home.

"It is small, but everyone is friendly and there are several couples here who are around our age."

I wonder where they live? There couldn't be more than a dozen houses in this entire town, Vivienne thought to herself.

"It's good to finally have you and the boys here. I've missed y'all," Diego told Vivienne later that evening, when they were sitting outside their new home watching the boys play.

"We've missed you terribly. The boys kept asking where you were and why you didn't come home. It was rather hard for me to explain to them."

"I know and I'm sorry. Now that we're all together, we can start enjoying each other again and get our lives back to normal.

"I missed you and the boys even more than I thought I was going to. Between trying to learn the terrain and getting to know the people in the area, I never thought much about anyone except the three of you. Since you've been here I've had time to think about the rest of the family. You know who I miss the most?"

"Victoria," Vivienne answered without stopping to think about the question.

"How did you know that?" he asked in surprise.

"Because the two of you are so much alike. And don't deny it. That's the reason you argue so much. You're both rather hot tempered and have trouble understanding how anyone can have a different view point on something other than the one you have. One of the things you miss most about your sister is not having someone to spar with."

"I guess you're right," he said thoughtfully. "If Victoria and I are close because we're so much alike, then why are you and I close? We're certainly not anything alike."

"I think I'm a challenge to you. I know you're certainly a challenge for me! And we're more alike than you may realize."

"Like how?"

"Family means a lot to both of us. We love our children and enjoy being with them, but we're both rather strict with them. Both of us enjoy being around people. Just to name a few things."

For two people who enjoy being with people, we're certainly living in a town where there won't be much socializing. *There are fewer people here than live on Black Creek*

Ranch, Vivienne thought. *I wonder if Diego is going to miss the companionship of other people as much as I am?*

"How about naming all the ways we're different?" Diego said.

"It would take me two days to do that," she laughed.

"Another similarity you missed is we both have a sense of humor.

"I've sometimes wondered how Mama puts up with Papa and his temper and teasing. I think I just figured out how she does it. Although Mama also has a rather fierce temper, I don't think she takes a lot of what Papa says or does too seriously. I know sometimes she just shakes her head at something he has said, whereas most wives would get angry," Diego said.

"In spite of your father's temper and impatience, he has a heart of gold. Whether you like to admit it or not, you too have those characteristics."

"Like father, like son," he said.

"From what I've heard about your father and his younger years, I think your mother is greatly responsible for calming his temper. And, fortunately, for all concerned, marriage to Cody has calmed Victoria down."

"I think having two children has helped also. Matthew is mild tempered like Cody, but Victoria spends a lot of her energy trying to keep Selena's temper, that is equal to her own, under control.

"It wasn't so long ago that Victoria pitched a fit because Papa wouldn't let her marry Cody. I think now everyone agrees that, when he finally consented to them marrying, it was one the wisest decisions he ever made."

"You're right about that," Vivienne said. "And since Miranda, instead of you, is the major influence in Antonio's life he has also settled down considerably."

"Are you saying I was a bad influence on my little brother?"

"Not exactly a bad influence. Let's just say you brought out the devil in him," she said smiling.

"At least Miguel and Noelle never gave our parents any trouble. Two out of five's not bad.

"I've met a family here I think you're really going to like," he said after awhile. "Teresa and Joaquin Navarro.

"They have two daughters who are a little older than Travis and a son Charlie Joe's age. They own and operate the General Store. He's also the postmaster."

"I'm going to the store tomorrow to stock up on groceries. I'll meet the Navarros then."

"Be sure to check our post office box while you're there.

"Are you expecting something?" she asked.

"No. I just like to check it every day."

"Now that the boys and I are here, how could the mail be all that interesting?" she teased.

"Just habit I guess."

The next day Vivienne took the boys for a walk so they could all get acquainted with the people and the town. She didn't know whether everyone was outside because of the heat or because they had heard the Ranger's family had made it to town and they wanted to meet them.

When they passed by the school, Travis asked when classes were going to start.

"I don't know. When we go to the store to get groceries, I'll find out."

"I wonder how many kids will be in the school?" he asked.

"From what I've seen of the town, I imagine about as many as there were at the school on Black Creek," she told him. She wondered if there would even be that many.

That evening when Diego came home for supper Vivienne told him, while they had been at the General Store, they had met Teresa and Joaquin. "You were right. I really do like both of them. I invited them and their family for supper Saturday night. Teresa didn't say anything, but I imagine you owe them a few meals."

At that, Diego just grinned.

"I talked to Teresa about the quality of the school. She said there was only a total of about twenty-five students in the school and only one teacher. I'm concerned about how good an education the boys will receive there."

"You may need to tutor the boys so they will get a good education while we're here," Diego said thoughtfully.

"I also met another rather interesting person today, Rafael Valverde."

"I hope you didn't believe anything he said," Diego laughed. "That man has a more vivid imagination than Charlie Joe."

"It didn't take long for me to figure that out. I invited him for supper tomorrow night. He seemed really grateful for the invitation."

"I'm sure he was. I don't think he eats anything that doesn't come directly out of a can. He is quite entertaining but I'm not sure I want the boys getting too friendly with him. There's no telling what they're liable to learn from him. Not to mention, his grammar leaves a lot to be desired," Diego said, shaking his head. "Maybe we should put the boys to bed early tomorrow night."

"I don't think that would do any good. You know they're going to eventually meet Rafael. It might as well be now rather than later," Vivienne laughed.

"I guess we do owe him a thank you dinner as well. He's the one who found this house for us and convinced the owner to sell it to me for much less than I expected to pay." He then proceeded to tell her about his first meeting with Rafael and a little about Lapopa.

"Lapopa. She sounds like someone else I need to meet. Maybe we should invite her for dinner also," Vivienne said playfully after he told her about the woman. "If I have my say, you'll never have that opportunity."

"Oh, don't be such an old fogy. I know women like her exist and they do have their good points. They make a lot of men happy."

Diego turned crimson, his mouth agape.

"Diego Black! I never thought I would see this day. I do believe I just embarrassed you." Vivienne laughed.

"You're not suppose to know about things like that."

"I wasn't raised under a rock," she said, placing a kiss on his cheek.

He didn't tell Vivienne that Lapopa still hadn't given up on propositioning him.

Chapter 3

"I'm so glad y'all could come tonight. I hope this will be the beginning of a long friendship for all of us," Vivienne said to the Navarros when they arrived for supper Saturday night.

"I'm sure it will be. Joaquin and Diego have already become *amigos* and I can tell Paco and your youngest son are going to be friends," Teresa said, as they watched Charlie Joe toss his ball to Paco.

"When I told Charlie Joe you had a son his age, he was thrilled. He was so glad to know he would have someone to play with besides Travis."

"From what Diego has told us about Charlie Joe, I'm afraid we're going to have to watch those two very closely. Paco is also full of mischief."

"These are our daughters, Juana and Evita," Teresa said introducing the two girls to her.

"I'm so glad to meet you. Diego has told me many nice things about each of you."

"Thank you, ma'am," they both said shyly. They tucked their heads in embarrassment over her compliment.

"Oh, thank you. You didn't need to bring anything for supper," Vivienne said, as Juana handed her a pie pan that was still warm from the oven.

"It was no trouble, I like to cook," Juana told her.

Vivienne lifted the lid off the pan and took a peek at the pie. "Oh, an apple pie! That's Diego's favorite," she said smiling. She politely ignored the blush on both girls' faces that deepened at her words.

"Knowing how much Diego likes sweets, I knew we couldn't have too many," Teresa added.

"Since you know about his liking for sweets, you probably also know his appetite, in general, is large. I want to thank you for having him for supper so often before I got here. He said he really appreciated it and that you are an excellent cook," Vivienne said. She invited them into the house.

"*Gracias, Senora.* We enjoyed having him. We all care for him very much," Teresa assured her.

"Juana and Evita always enjoy having a handsome man sitting across the table from them. I think they're both secretly in love with him," she added with a chuckle.

The shy girls blushed again.

When they sat down at the table everyone began talking at once. It was as though they had known each other for years.

"Diego told me the two of you are from Mexico City. What brought you to Apache Flats?" Vivienne asked.

"That's an easy question to answer. I was the youngest of eleven children and I wanted to get as far away as I could from all those people telling me what to do," Joaquin said. Everyone laughed.

"After Teresa and I married, we set out for Texas," he continued. "We had no idea where we would end up. We agreed before leaving Mexico City that wherever we were in two weeks, after crossing the Rio Grande, is where we would settle. When the two weeks were up, we found ourselves here. Before we left Mexico, Teresa's father had given us some money to get started in our new country. Fortunately for us, the man who owned the General Store was wanting to sell it, so he could move to Ysleta where his daughter lived. We bought the store and have been here ever since.

"Since my English was good and no one else wanted the job, I was made postmaster. That extra income has enabled us to slowly buy ranchland. I plan to eventually put some sheep on the land, move out there and become a rancher."

"When you do that maybe you can go into the horse breeding business with me. My family owns and breeds some of the best horses in Bexar County. I plan to ask my father to send me a couple so I can start breeding. I've noticed the area could use some good horses," Diego said.

"That is true," Joaquin said. "Most of the horses around here are from horses the Spaniards brought when they first came to America. The only ones that were left were ones that escaped captivity and formed bands of wild horses. Most of them are rather small and hard to train.

"When you get the horses you are more than welcome to keep them on our *ranchero*."

"Thank you. I'll take you up on that offer."

"Have you met Raul Hidalgo?" Joaquin asked.

"No. I don't believe I have."

"He has a large sheep ranch south of town. If you get your horses before we move to our *ranchero* I'm certain he will be glad to keep them on his land, for a small fee."

"Thanks. I'll look into that," Diego said.

"Vivienne, Diego told us your family had a sheep ranch when you were a girl," Joaquin said, turning his attention to her.

"Yes, but we only spent the summers on the ranch. The rest of the year we lived in Wolf Creek, where my father was the marshal, so we could go to school. When Diego and I married, we moved to San Pablo. Shortly after that my parents moved to a house on Diego's family's ranch, which is very close to San Pablo. My father then became the marshal in San Pablo."

"My goodness," Teresa said. "There are certainly a lot of lawmen in your family."

"Yes, there are. And Charlie Joe claims he's going to be Texas Ranger when he grows up," Diego told her.

"Diego, may I ask you a very personal question?" Teresa asked hesitantly.

"Of course," he said.

"I have been wondering since I first met you, how you came to have a Spanish given name."

"That's a question I'm asked frequently," Diego said with a smile. "My mother's parents came over here from Spain soon after they married.

"Shortly after they came to America, and before either of our parents were born, they were on their way to Texas and stopped in a small town in Virginia. By chance while they were there, they met my father's parents. After my parents married my grandmother got to thinking about some of the things my father had told her about my mother and her parents. She realized the families had met years before."

"My goodness. It is a small world," Teresa commented.

"Before my older brother was born, Papa said he liked the Spanish names better than the English ones. So they named him Miguel. My younger brother is named Antonio. However, my twin sisters don't have Spanish names. Victoria was named for my father's grandmother and Noelle got her name because they were born on Christmas."

"And, I'm named after a famous Texas Ranger, Joseph Travis!" Travis told them proudly.

"And when I grow up I'm going to be a Texas Ranger, just like Papa and Ranger Travis," Charlie Joe informed them, trying to outdo his brother.

Not if I have anything to say about it, Vivienne thought to herself. *I don't think I could bear having a husband and a son both being Rangers.*

"Speaking of being a Ranger, you told me that Ranger Travis was the one who inspired you to become a Ranger. Besides his recommendation, what did you have to do to become a Ranger? I have heard it is very hard to be appointed," Joaquin asked.

"Well, first, you have to be able to take orders without questioning them, and, second, you have to be able to give orders in a manner that will not be questioned. My father was a good teacher as far as giving orders that had best be obeyed. My family has told me I'm good at giving orders," he said as he looked at Vivienne and grinned.

"If he gives us an order and we don't obey, we get a whipping," Charlie Joe told them.

"Yes, and sometimes you still don't obey," Diego said, looking at his son and raising his eyebrows.

Charlie Joe just looked down at his plate and didn't say anymore.

"Right after Vivienne and I married I became her father's deputy marshal. The two years experience I had working with him was in my favor for being appointed to the Rangers," Diego told him.

"It also didn't hurt to be recommended by a famous, respected Ranger who had known me since I was five years old," he admitted.

"It sounds like you were destined to become a Ranger. From what I have seen of how you operate and how you handle a gun, El Paso County is very lucky to have you," Joaquin said.

"Thank you. My father's the one who taught me how to handle a gun. His accuracy with a rifle and a pistol and his fast draw are as good as mine."

"Did your father ever think about becoming a lawman?" Joaquin asked.

"No. He enjoys ranching too much to ever think about doing anything else."

"Your apple pie is delicious," Vivienne told Juana, as they were eating dessert.

"Thank you, ma'am," she replied shyly.

"Yes. It is every bit as good as your mother's," Diego told her.

"Thank you, sir," Juana said, as a deep blush again crossed her face.

I wonder if Evita and Juana are always this quiet or if it's because Diego is here? Teresa was right about them being secretly in love with him. Neither of them have been able to take their eyes off of him since, they got here. I wonder if he's noticed? Probably not, Vivienne reasoned.

The rest of the evening the two families spent visiting and

getting better acquainted.

"Good evening, Captain Jones," Diego said one evening a couple of weeks later, when he answered the knock at the door. "What brings you to Apache Flats? Is there trouble?"

"Not that I know of," the captain said with a wide smile. "I heard your family had finally made it out here. I came to meet them."

"Yes. I'm happy to say they're here. Come in and let me introduce you.

"This is my wife, Vivienne, and these are our sons, Travis and Charlie Joe," Diego said.

As they were talking the captain removed his hat.

"You don't have any hair!" Charlie Joe said in surprise, as he looked at the top of the captain's head.

"Charlie Joe, that wasn't nice!" Vivienne reprimanded him, as a blush crossed her face at her son's words.

The captain took the remark just as Diego was sure he would. He looked at Charlie Joe with a twinkle in his eyes, and said, "That's all right, ma'am. I like a man who says what's on his mind."

"I'm afraid you'll find that youngest son of ours is like me, and, more often than not, speaks before he thinks," Diego said.

"Never apologize for the actions of another man. Even a young one. It's all right to call them down for their words or actions, but don't apologize for them," the captain told him.

"I'm sorry I said that, Captain. I didn't mean to hurt your feelings."

"Your apology is accepted," the captain said with a smile.

"Captain Jones, your timing is very good. Supper is almost ready," Vivienne said.

"I wouldn't want to put you out, ma'am, but that does sounds mighty inviting."

"It's no trouble. There's plenty. We're glad to have you."

"Okay, you two run along now. I'll call ya'll when it's time to eat," Vivienne told Travis and Charlie Joe.

"I'm very pleased to meet you, Captain. Diego has told me some very nice things about you. You just proved to me you are a gentleman with a sense of humor."

"The pleasure is all mine," he said as he looked at Vivienne and smiled. "Lieutenant, I'm glad to see you weren't exaggerating when you told me your wife was beautiful."

"Thank you, Captain! You are also quite the charmer," Vivienne said.

"I never say anything that's not the truth."

"Diego, if you will show Captain Jones into the sitting room, I'll check on supper."

"Captain Jones, do you have any children?" Travis asked when they were all seated around the dining room table.

"Yes. I have a daughter who's fifteen."

"What's her name?" Travis asked.

"Louise."

"Another characteristic our children have is they're both full of questions," Diego said.

"That's good. They'll learn a lot that way. If you think they ask a lot of questions, you should have a daughter. I swear the first two words out of Louise's mouth that went together when she learned to talk were in the form of a question. In fact, until just recently, every other sentence of hers was a question," the captain told him.

"Vivienne, I'm afraid you're going to find yourself embarrassed more often than not if you let these boys embarrass you every time they ask someone a personal question. I'm sure Diego managed to embarrass his mother more than a few times when he was a boy."

"Mama said I was the world's worst at asking questions and saying things I shouldn't. Fortunately, for her, she didn't embarrass as easily as Vivienne does." Diego laughed, as he winked at Vivienne.

"Just the other day, you told me I was beautiful when I blush," she teased.

"Are you telling me you sometimes feign embarrassment

to get a compliment?”

"The three of you manage to genuinely embarrass me often enough; I never have to pretend," she laughed.

CHAPTER 4

What sort of problem could Sheriff Addison possibly have that he needs my help with? Generally he can handle any situation that comes up. His telegraph, "I need your help," didn't tell me a damn thing, Diego thought as he rode along the trail to Bentley.

"Morning, Sheriff," Diego said when he walked into the sheriff's office the next morning and saw the sheriff sitting at his desk. "Now that I'm here, are you going to tell me why you need my help?"

"Howdy, Ranger," the sheriff answered. "Thanks for comin'. Sure sorry 'bout the short telegram. I didn't want nobody to find out why I was askin' fer yer help. Ya' know there's a big trial comin' up in Ben Ficklin next week. A man here in Bentley, by the name of Isaiah Nelson, has some important information he wants to give at the trial.

"Since I ain't got a deputy no more, I can't leave here to take Mr. Nelson to Ben Ficklin. I need your help gittin' him there safe 'n sound. I know yer better at protectin' people than me. If certain people find out 'bout the information he's got, they'll try to kill him."

"Has he told you what the information is?"

"Yep, and I ain't got no doubt he's tellin' the truth. What he knows will definitely send the man to prison for a long time."

"All right, I'll take him. But, I'd like to talk to him before we go."

"I can git him here in ten minutes. I know he's at home. He ain't left his house since he told me about the information he wants to give at the trial."

"Just tell me where he lives and I'll go talk to him. We don't want a prime witness getting shot before he has a chance to testify," Diego said. He removed his badge and put it in his pocket.

When he got to the address the sheriff had given him and knocked on the door, he saw someone carefully draw the curtain back and a man's face peered from behind it. Diego slowly moved his hand to his pocket, pulled out his badge and showed it to the man. With that, the curtain fell back in place and the door opened.

"I'm Texas Ranger Diego Black. Sheriff Addison tells me you have some information you need to give at the trial in Ben Ficklin."

"Yes sir, I do. Thanks for coming. I'm Isaiah Nelson," the man said as Diego stepped inside. He quickly shut the door behind him. Nelson was a rather heavy set man with a pock marked face; he appeared to be in his early fifties.

"I'll be forever grateful if you can get me to Ben Ficklin safe 'n sound. Sit down and I'll tell you what I know about Kirby Blake and why I need to testify at his trial," Nelson said.

"I would say that's information more people than just Blake would pay dearly to make certain never reaches the courtroom," Diego said after listening to what Nelson had to say. "When does the next stage to Ben Ficklin leave here?"

"We're in luck. The stage comes through at ten o'clock. It passes right by here on the way to the relay station so we can wait here. It's half-past nine now, so we shouldn't have long to wait," he said looking at the clock. "The station is just down the street."

"Good. I'll go now to get our tickets and stop by the sheriff's office to let him know when we're going. Then I'll come back here and wait for the stagecoach with you.

"Don't mention you're going to Ben Ficklin for the trial.

If anyone asks, you're headed for San Angelo and don't say anything about me being a Texas Ranger. For your safety I'd like to keep that information from getting out."

When they heard the stagecoach pass by, they got up and quickly went to the relay station.

"I'll be watching everyone on the stage with us," Diego quietly assured Isaiah, as they watched the other passengers get into the coach. "I want you to do the same."

"There are only three others who will be in the coach and one of them is a woman," Nelson said

"Never under estimate a woman," Diego said quietly. "In case you didn't notice, one of the pockets on her skirt has something rather large and heavy in it. My guess is she's toting a gun.

"I want to sit across from her. So you board first and take the seat next to her."

After they had been traveling for a while Diego pulled his hat down over his face and his eyes seemed to be closed. To the other passengers in the coach he appeared to be asleep but, through a slit in his eyelids, he was carefully watching all of them, especially the woman.

He had about given up on anyone making a suspicious move when he saw the woman slowly move her hand to her right pocket as though she was scratching her leg. When her hand disappeared into the pocket, Diego decided it was time to take action.

"Texas Ranger," Diego said. He quickly drew his gun and pointed it at her. "Slowly remove the gun from your pocket and put it on your lap. And don't try anything. If you should, I'll be shooting to kill. And at this close range, I can't miss."

The woman was obviously startled by his words but did as

he had told her. Sure enough, she pulled out a large shiny, new Colt .45 from her pocket.

"Thank you. It seems we have a prisoner," he said. He smiled at Isaiah as he picked the gun up.

"I thought you was asleep," the woman snarled.

"A Ranger never sleeps on the job," Diego said.

"Now do you want to tell me why you attempted to pull the gun?" he asked.

"I ain't telling you nothin'," she retorted.

"Fine. In the meantime, Isaiah, while I keep my gun trained on her, will you tie her hands behind her?" Diego asked. He pulled a short piece of rope from his pocket.

"Not everyone keeps a rope in their pocket," Isaiah said.

"I try to always be prepared."

When the woman's hands were securely tied behind her, one of the other passengers spoke up. "I didn't say anything earlier because I was afraid to, but her name is Bella Gates. She's a friend of Kirby Blake's and she's meaner than hell. If you arrest her, it won't be her first time in jail."

"Well, well. Bella Gates. I've heard of you, but I never thought I'd have the pleasure of meeting you," Diego said.

Her lips puckered at his remark, and for a moment, he thought she was going to spit at him.

That evening as the coach approached the relay station and slowed down, Diego looked at the other passengers and said, "The lady and I are going to get out here. I want the rest of you to stay in the coach until I tell you it's safe. I have a feeling some of her friends will be here to greet us."

"Okay, Bella," Diego said when the coach came to a stop, "you can get out now. But remember, I'm right behind you with a gun at your back."

As she stepped down from the coach, she yelled, "Texas Ranger!"

Diego had a firm grip on her arm. When she tried to pull away and duck she was unable to do so. Apparently the man who had been leaning against the front of the relay station thought she was going to duck because his bullet, which was intended for Diego, hit her instead.

As Diego let go of her arm, her lifeless body fell to the ground and he aimed his gun at the man who had shot her. Diego's aim was good. The man's gun was knocked from his hand before he could fire again.

At the same time, a second shot was heard. The shotgun rider on the coach had shot another man who had also drawn on Diego.

When the shooting was over, Diego asked the shotgun rider to watch the wounded outlaw while he checked inside the station office. He went inside and discovered the two outlaws had killed the station manager before the coach had arrived. He went back outside and told the passengers it was now safe to get out of the coach while the driver changed horses, but warned them not to go into the station.

"It looks like we have three dead bodies as well as a prisoner. After you change horses and take the passengers into Ben Ficklin, would you ask Sheriff Blair to bring a wagon out here? Isaiah and I will stay with the prisoner and the bodies until the sheriff gets here," Diego instructed the driver after he told them about the station manager.

"Thanks for taking care of that man for me," he told the shotgun rider. "How did you know to shoot him and not me?" Diego asked.

"I seen his picture on a wanted poster a few days back and knew he was a wanted man. And, I was in Ysleta a couple of months ago when you stopped that bank robbery. I knew you was a Ranger.

"I didn't say nothin' to you when I seen you back in Bentley because I seen you wasn't wearing a badge. I knew there musta' been a reason for that."

"Thanks for being so observant. I don't think I could have taken care of both of those men before they killed someone else."

"I think you could 'ave. That day in Ysleta, it was just you against three armed men and you took 'em all three without no trouble. You're mighty handy with a gun."

"I appreciate your confidence, but that day I had the protection of a building and I was using a rifle."

"Well, you done a fine job taking care of them three."

"Thank you. I'd appreciate it if you would watch out for the passengers while the driver changes horses," Diego said.

With that he took the prisoner over to where Isaiah was waiting. "I suppose we should take care of the prisoner's wound," Diego said, as they went into the relay station.

"If you'll keep your gun on him, I'll dress his wound," Isaiah said. "I had some experience doing that during the war."

After the prisoner's wound was tended, Diego tied the man to a chair and he and Isaiah sat down to wait for the sheriff.

"I don't suppose you've also had experience cooking have you?" he asked Isaiah.

"Some. I'll see what I can rustle us up to eat," he said. He went to the other side of the room and began searching through the cabinets.

"What about me? You gonna' let me starve?" the prisoner whined.

"As much as I'd like to, I guess when it's time, I'll tether one of your hands long enough for you to eat."

"You think the sheriff will be here tonight?" Isaiah asked, as he stoked up a fire in the stove and began opening cans and pouring the contents into the pots he had found.

"Hopefully. I'm not looking forward to sitting here all night with a gun pointed at this *hombre*."

When they finished eating Diego took the dishes to the sink and washed them. He then lit a lantern and they settled down to wait for the sheriff. They had about decided he wasn't coming until morning when they heard a wagon approaching the cabin. Going outside, Diego was surprised to see not one, but two men in the wagon.

"Captain Jones! I certainly didn't expect to see you to-night. Thanks for coming."

"Lieutenant, this is Sheriff Blair. I was in his office when the driver of the stagecoach came in and said there was a Texas Ranger and another man at the relay station with a prisoner and three dead bodies. You want to tell me what's going on?"

"Captain, Sheriff Blair, this is Isaiah Nelson. He has some valuable information about Kirby Blake that should send the man to prison for a long time. I'm trying to get him safely to Ben Ficklin so he can testify at the trial," Diego explained. They entered the cabin and Diego continued. "Thank you both for coming. I don't know how many others there might be who will try to keep us from reaching Ben Ficklin.

"Isaiah, this is my boss, Captain T. P. Jones, Texas Ranger and this is Sheriff Blair, sheriff of Tom Green County.

"We've had a little trouble. Before we got here this *hombre* and his friend killed the station manager. Then, when we were getting out of the stagecoach, he shot at me. His bullet missed and killed the woman I had just taken into custody. She was none other than Bella Gates. The shotgun rider on the stagecoach killed the other outlaw."

"I've had dealings with Bella," Sheriff Blair told them, as he looked at Bella's body. "She was as mean and ornery as any man I've come across. You're lucky you lived to find out who she was.

"Her two partners here are both wanted for murder and several robberies. Looks like we'll be having a hanging as well as three funerals," the sheriff added as he turned his look to the man who was tied to the chair. "Sounds like y'all had a busy afternoon. I notice you aren't wearing your badge," the captain said, to Diego.

"I was hoping, if no one knew I was an officer of the law, word wouldn't get out there was an important witness on his way to Ben Ficklin. Unfortunately, the plan didn't work," Diego said. He took the badge out of his pocket and pinned it to his shirt.

"It was a good plan," the captain said. "Sometimes even

the best of plans don't turn out the way we expect."

"Captain, I'll go into Ben Ficklin with you tonight, but I'd like to head on back home in the morning if you don't need me after that. I need to get back to my territory."

"Is it your territory or your pretty little wife you want to get back to?" the captain asked with a grin.

"Both," Diego admitted guiltily.

"I think Sheriff Blair and I can handle the situation. After we get this man to town and in the jail, you can go on back home. Give Vivienne my regards."

"Thank you, sir. I will."

It was late the next night when Diego got home. He walked quietly down the hall and looked in each of the boys' rooms and found they were both sound asleep.

When he went into his and Vivienne's bedroom, she was sitting up in bed. "Welcome home," she said smiling.

"Thanks. It's good to be home," he answered with a tired smile. He sat down on the edge of the bed. After giving Vivienne a long, hungry kiss, he began undressing.

"How did it go?"

"Interesting. I'll tell you about it in the morning."

"Before I forget, Joaquin came by yesterday and said to tell you he needs to talk to you."

"Did he say what about?"

"No."

"Well, whatever he needs will have to wait until morning. I'm exhausted. But, I'm not too tired to take care of our needs," he said with a smile, as he pulled his boots off. He then removed the rest of his clothes and tossed them on the floor on top of his boots. Lying down, he took her in his arms.

"Are you ever too tired for that?" she asked.

"Never," he answered, as he slipped her gown off her shoulders. As his hands began roaming her body, his lips ran trails of kisses down her neck.

"I'm hungry for you," he said. He began to nibble on her ear.

"Oh, that feels good," Vivienne said breathlessly, as she felt his shaft enter her.

CHAPTER 5

"Good morning," Diego said, the next morning as he entered the General Store.

"*Buenos dias amigo,* and welcome home," Joaquin answered.

"Thanks. It's good to be home. Vivienne said you needed to talk to me."

"*Si. Senor* Mateo Gomez was in here Thursday and told me he was going to be leaving the area. When I asked why, he said he couldn't afford to stay any longer. After talking to him awhile, he finally told me his sheep were being poisoned."

"How long has that been going on?" Diego asked.

"From what he said, since last fall."

"Why hasn't he said anything to me about it?"

"I asked him that and he said, Texas Rangers don't have time to worry about a poor Mexican sheep man."

"Damn! When are people around here going to be convinced I don't care who they are or how much or how little money they have. I'm here to protect everyone."

"It may take you a while to do that. The Ranger who was here before you seemed to be only interested in protecting men who had money."

"Well, that's not the way I operate. I'm here for everybody." *Now I know for certain that was the reason the last Ranger was transferred back to San Antonio headquarters and a desk job*, Diego thought.

"Does he have any idea who's doing it?"

"That is the problem. He is almost certain it is one of *Senor* Colton's *vaquero's*. He said Colton has been trying to get him to sell him his ranch for the past year.

"In case you haven't heard, Colton's been quietly threatening all the small ranchers in the area ever since he's been here. None of them will openly admit it, but they are all afraid of him."

"No one has come out and told me that but I've heard rumors to that affect. I guess they all thought I would defend Colton."

After going by the house to tell Vivienne he would be gone for a couple of days and where he would be, he rode out to the Gomez ranch.

"*Buenas diaz, Senor* Gomez," Diego said when he saw the man later that morning. "I hear you've lost some sheep to poison over the past months."

"*Si, Senor* Ranger."

"Do you know who's doing it?"

"*Hago no sabe, Senor.*"

"*Senor* Gomez, *por favor*, be completely honest with me. I'm here to protect you from anyone who is trying to do you harm. I don't care who that someone might be. I want to see him brought to justice."

He remained silent as he studied Diego, trying to decide if he meant what he had said. Finally Gomez replied, "*Si Senor. Le creo. Que es Senor* Colton."

"There is a watering tank over there," he said, pointing to a windmill about a mile from the house. "Each evening I turn off the windmill and empty the tank. One of *Senor* Colton's men comes at night and turns the windmill on and puts poison in the tank."

"Does he come every night?"

"*Si, Senor.*"

"I'm going back to town and have someone come back

out here with me and take my horse back to town so there won't be any evidence I'm here. Then, after dark, I'll hide in the draw over there and wait for the man to come, so I can catch him in the act and arrest him."

"*Muchas gracias, Senor* Ranger," Gomez said.

When Diego got back to Apache Flats that afternoon he went to the room where Rafael lived, but he wasn't there. *Well, Rafael,* he thought, *it's a little early in the day, but I'll be willing to bet I know where I can find you.* Sure enough, when he went into the saloon he saw Rafael sitting at a table talking to Lapopa.

"Rafael, I need to talk to you about something rather important," Diego said, as he sat down at the table and cast a quick look at Lapopa.

"Huh! I know when I ain't wanted," Lapopa grunted as she got up and abruptly left the table.

"Rafael," Diego said when Lapopa was out of hearing, "you've been telling me you would like to help me sometime. If you were serious about that, I can use your help today."

"*Si, Senor.* What do ya' want me to do?" Rafael asked.

"Someone's been poisoning Mateo Gomez' sheep. I'm going back out to his ranch now and, hopefully, tonight I'll catch the man who's been doing it. I want you to go with me and bring my horse back to town. I won't be back until tomorrow, but I'll tell Vivienne to expect you for supper tonight.

"Then I would like for you to go to the jail and stay for the night. I'm almost certain I'll be bringing back a prisoner. I'll deputize you so you can guard him tonight."

Those words brought a proud smile to Rafael's face. "Do you know who the prisoner will be?" Rafael asked after they went to the jail and he had been deputized.

When Diego told him it would most likely be one of Terence Colton's men, Rafael said, "*Senor* Colton's men do not do nothing that he does not tell them to do."

"We'll have to ride fast. I want you to get back to town with my horse before any of Colton's men see you."

"Do not worry. My horse can keep up with yer fine steed." With that, he went to get his horse. "Ya' sure ya' do not want me to stay with ya' tonight? There may be more than one *hombre*," Rafael asked as they rode out of town.

"Thanks for the offer, but since Mateo doesn't have a barn for me to put my horse in and there's no place on the ranch to hide him, it's important you take him back to town. I don't want anyone to know I'm there. I'm certain the one who is doing the poisoning won't come if he sees another horse on the ranch."

"How ya' gonna get back to town?" Rafael asked.

"I'll ride the prisoner's horse and he can ride Mateo's horse."

"You think *Senor* Colton's *hombre* will have a better *caballo* than *Senor* Gomez's *caballo*?" Rafael asked with a smile.

"I know he will," Diego answered.

That evening, as Diego settled himself in the shallow draw to wait for the man who would, hopefully, come early, he looked around at his surroundings. *Not only is this the most uncomfortable place I've ever sat, I'm open range to every rattlesnake, wolf and coyote that should happen by,* he thought. *I can't even shoot them without giving my presence away.*

About midnight, as he was watching another rattlesnake slither past, he heard a horse come up to the tank. Turning quietly and slowly, so as not to alert his presence to the man or the snake, he raised up just enough to peer over the top of the draw. He saw a man, who had his back to him, start up the windmill and empty something into the tank.

He sat up quickly and went to where the man was standing. The squeaking of the turning windmill muffled any sound Diego made, enabling him to sneak up behind him without being heard. He put his gun to the man's back, and quietly said, "Texas Ranger. Don't turn around. Just put your hands behind you so I can tie them together." He then pulled a piece of rope from his pocket and tied the man's hands behind him. He then removed the man's gun from it's holster and put it under his own gun belt.

"You're one of Colton's men, aren't you?"

The man didn't say anything.

"Now, start walking to the house over there, "Diego ordered.

"I can't walk that far. It's over a mile. I suppose you're going to ride my horse," the man sneered.

"Oh, I think you can. Remember, I'm the one with the gun, so you'll do as I say and, you're right, I am going to ride your horse."

After going to Mateo's house to let him know the man had been caught and to get his horse so the prisoner could ride back to town, they helped him mount.

"*Gracias, Senor* Ranger," Mateo said. "He is one of *Senor* Colton's *hombres*."

"I thought so. Now the next thing I need to do is arrest Colton. Thanks for the use of your horse. I'll have someone bring him back to you later today." With that, the Ranger and the prisoner headed to Apache Flats and the jail.

When Diego got to the jail, Rafael was waiting for him. It didn't take long for the two of them to get a confession out of the man that Colton was the one who had paid him to poison the water.

Afterwards, Diego headed back to Colton's ranch to arrest him. The sun had just come over the horizon when he saw Colton and another man riding toward Mateo Gomez' ranch. He rode up behind the two men, pulled his gun and commanded, "Texas Ranger. Stop right there, Colton. You're under arrest."

At his order, Colton's hired gun turned and pulled his weapon. Before he had a chance to shoot, Diego fired, knocking the man from the saddle.

"All right, Colton, unless you want to meet the same fate as your friend there, I suggest you drop your gun," Diego said, as he turned his gun toward Colton.

When Colton dropped his gun onto the dirt, Diego said, "Now get off your horse and get your friend's gun and toss it over there, next to yours."

Colton went to the man and rolled him over so he could get the gun. As he picked up the six shooter, he remarked, "He's dead."

"Then put him across his saddle. Remember, on the ride to the jail, I'll have my gun pointed at your back," Diego told him, as he dismounted and picked up the guns.

After taking Colton to the jail and the dead man to the undertaker, Diego headed home.

"What's wrong?" Vivienne asked when he came into the house and she saw the expression on his face.

He slowly removed his gun belt and put it across the back of the kitchen chair. Then, he took a deep breath and sat down heavily. "I just killed a man. I've shot several men but that's the first time I ever killed anyone."

"Oh, Diego, I'm sorry. I know that part of your job is going to be the hardest on you," Vivienne said. She sat down next to him and put her hand on his.

"I guess I'd better get use to it. I'm sure he's not the last man I'll have to kill. He was a hired gun working for Colton. There's no telling how many men he'd killed. He probably deserved to die. But, somehow, that thought doesn't make it any easier on me."

"I once heard my father say that sometimes criminals intentionally put themselves in the line of fire because they would rather face death than the hangman's noose or spend time in prison."

"That's an interesting viewpoint," he said.

They sat in silence for several minutes before Diego got

up from his chair. "I guess I'd better put it behind me and go on."

"I wish there was something else I could do or say to put your mind at ease," Vivienne said sympathetically.

"There's nothing anyone can do. As you said, that's part of being a Ranger. It's between the lawman in me and my conscience. Just be here for me and love me," he said. He placed a kiss on her cheek.

"I'll always love you and be here for you," she said.

"Some things never change," Seth said, as he walked into the house. "We just got a six page letter from Diego and I can't read a word he's written."

"Oh here, let me have it," Maria said, taking the letter from him.

"You don't need to read me the whole thing. Just tell me what he wants this time."

"If I'm going to read it, you're going to hear all of it," Maria told him.

"In other words, if I want to find out what he wants, I'll have to suffer through it with you," he complained.

"Just be glad one of our children writes. Diego's written more letters than the other four put together. And, as I've told you before, his penmanship isn't any worse than yours.

"'I'm finding the horses out here are of very poor stock,'" she read. "'The best of them aren't as good as the worst horse in the entire county of Bexar. If you have any horses you can part with, would you please send them to me? I'll take anything you have. I think I'd like to start a breeding ranch out here. There won't be any money in it but good horses are really needed.'"

"Well, for once, he didn't waste any time letting us know what he wants. Has he ever written when he didn't ask for something?" Seth grumbled.

"Oh, be quiet and let me finish the letter," Maria said. "In the first place, he's not asking for something for himself.

He's simply trying to better the grade of horses in the area."

"Ha! He's asking because he wants to raise horses," Seth said as he started out of the room. "And you can be sure, he'll find a way to turn it into a money maker."

"Don't you want to hear the rest of the letter?"

"I've heard all I need to. I've got to go pick out the horses to send him. I can think of four off hand I can part with, but I need to talk to Cody first."

"You're right, dear husband, some things never change. You have yet to listen to one of Diego's letters to the end," Maria called after him, with a smile.

"Why should I? If he has anything important to say, you'll tell me," Seth said, turning to return her smile.

"Well, Cody and I are in agreement about the horses to send," Seth said when he came in for supper that evening. We picked out three broodmares, all of which are in foal, and that young bay stallion. He should make a good stud. Next year Diego can breed him to the mares I'm sending. This year he should be able to make some money breeding him to mares in their area.

"Letting Victoria marry Cody was the best thing we ever did. Not only has he calmed down that headstrong daughter of ours, he's the main reason we have one of the best horse breeding ranches in the county. I wonder if him being part Indian has anything to do with the uncanny way he has with horses? They seem to understand every word he says.

"I'm also sending a couple of geldings I haven't been able to sell. If the horses out there are as bad a stock as Diego claims, he shouldn't have any trouble selling them. Don't worry, I'll let him have them for a fair price."

"Seth!"

"Oh, I suppose you think I should let him have them for nothing," he grinned.

"I not only think you should, I know you will!"

"Even though they're the bottom line of our horses, I can't

trust anyone with taking them that distance. I guess I'll have to take them myself," Seth grumbled again. "I thought I'd leave sometime next week. Do you want to go with me?"

"You know I do!"

"If you're planning to go, you'll probably want to take at least one trunk full of stuff for them. So, I'd better plan on taking our coach.

"I'm not about to let those horses be herded all that way. I don't want every bandit and horse thief between here and Apache Flats to see them. As soon as I find a driver and someone to ride shotgun on our coach, we can leave. Hopefully, I'll be able to find someone with a closed in coach who will be willing to transport the horses that distance. It sure would make things easier if the train went as far as Apache Flats."

"You could always build a coach to transport the horses."

"I could, but I don't want to. That would take too long."

"I'll get our things packed and be ready to go whenever you're ready to leave. Before you do anything else will you get the two large trunks out of the attic?"

Chapter 6

"We got a letter from your mother today," Vivienne told Diego. "She and your father are coming for a visit. They'll arrive about the tenth of next month."

"Did she say if they're going to bring any horses?" he asked anxiously.

"If I say no, are you still going to be glad to see them?"

"Of course!"

"She didn't say how long they will be able to stay. Will you be able to spend at least a few uninterrupted days with them?"

"I'll try my best. They'll be here for two weeks," he told her.

"How do you know that?"

"Because, Mama will want to stay a month and Papa will want to stay two days. So, they'll compromise and stay two weeks."

"When I told the boys their grandparents were coming for a visit, they were so excited they could hardly eat their lunch. They miss them so much."

"Since you didn't answer my question, I don't know how many horses Papa is bringing. I guess I should start making plans now to build another stable."

"What makes you so sure he's bringing any?" Vivienne teased.

"Because, if he weren't, you would have said so. I am right, aren't I?" he asked grinning.

"Yes. You know me too well. They're bringing six."

"Oh! That's more than I dared hope for. I'll have to start finding the lumber to build the stable. Lumber is more scarce out here than rain."

"You'll be happy to know your father is sending enough lumber to build the stable. Your mother said it should be here about the time they arrive. She also said they're bringing the plans Miguel drew for the stable."

"Good. When they get here Papa can help me build it. In the meantime, I'd better get busy putting up a corral to keep the horses in until the stable's built."

"Have you talked to Raul about boarding the horses on his ranch?" she asked.

"Yes. He said he'll be glad to keep them. Before you ask, I told him I'd pay him. This had better be a money making project," Diego added.

"Do you think Raul will object to you building a stable large enough to accommodate all those horses on his ranch?"

"Not if we make it large enough for him to keep his horses in it too. The barn he has now is about to fall down, it's in such bad condition."

"How was your first morning of school?" Vivienne asked Charlie Joe when the boys came home for lunch.

"Terrible! I had to sit in a chair all morning and I couldn't even talk unless I raised my hand and asked Mr. Barnes if I could. And I didn't even learn anything! Do I have to go back this afternoon?"

"Yes, you do. The first day is usually just so everyone can get acquainted and get use to being in school.

"Actually, you did learn something. You learned to sit quietly all morning and to ask permission to talk or to get out of your chair. I'm proud of you. And, I'm sure you made some new friends," his mother told him.

"How was the morning for you?" she asked Travis, knowing his answer would be entirely different from his brother's.

"There are two boys who weren't there last year. One of them is ten years old but he's in the same grade I am. He said his family moves around a lot so he hasn't been able to go to school very much. He doesn't know a lot of English, so he has trouble in school."

"I hope you'll be nice to him and help him with his school work," Vivienne suggested.

"I like him a lot. I think he's real poor. He doesn't have any shoes."

"Maybe you can invite him to come play with you one Saturday morning and you can spend the day together." *If the boy doesn't have shoes, he probably doesn't have enough to eat either,* Vivienne thought to herself.

"How much longer until Grandma and Grandpa get here?" Travis asked excitedly.

"They'll be here in four or five days," Maria told him.

"Do we have to go to school while they're here?" Charlie Joe asked hopefully.

"You most certainly do."

"Oh," he replied disappointedly.

Vivienne could barely suppress a smile at the disappointed look on her younger son's face.

"I'm so glad to see you!" Vivienne said a few days later when the coach pulled up in front of the house and Seth and Maria got out. "And you're a day earlier than we expected," she said as she and Maria hugged.

"I added a couple of extra days to when you might expect us, so you wouldn't worry. I hope our being early doesn't conflict with any plans you have," Maria said.

"Not at all. We're glad to see you anytime you can be here."

"Before I do anything else I'm going to get a hug from this beautiful lady," Seth said, as he came over to where Maria and Vivienne were standing.

"I've missed you. Diego may not tell you, but he's also missed you," Vivienne told him as they hugged.

"I'll have to admit, I've missed him too," he told her. With that he went back to the coach to help unload the horses.

"I'm so anxious to see the boys. It's been over a year since we've seen them. I know they've changed a lot in that time."

"Yes, they have. Especially Charlie Joe. He's now as tall as Travis and he's slimmed down a lot. He still looks more like me than Travis does, but I think he's going to be tall and well built like Diego. He started school this month and just as we expected, he thinks it a total waste of his time.

"They're both anxious to see the two of you. They've missed you so much. Ever since we got your letter telling us when to expect you, they've talked about little else."

As they talked, the drivers of the two coaches who had brought Maria, Seth and the horses, took two trunks off the top of the coach and put them on the ground next to where Vivienne and Maria were standing.

"My goodness, you certainly brought enough stuff," Vivienne laughed.

"It took her a week to gather all the stuff she wanted to bring. For a while I thought we were going to have to bring the wagon as well, to carry everything," Seth remarked.

Maria just looked at him and shook her head, but otherwise ignored his statement.

"The large black trunk contains things for the four of you," Maria told her. "There are several bolts of material for you to make yourself some dresses and some shirts for the boys. There are also some toys and other things for the boys. I found a new game called Tiddley Winks I thought the boys would like. Even though I thought the six horses were enough for Diego, I couldn't resist bringing him a belt I found.

"I also brought several school books the school on Black Creek isn't using anymore. Do you think the school here might find them useful?"

"Oh, yes. Thank you! We are always in need of school books. The area is so poor some of the children have to share textbooks. The excellent school on Black Creek is one of the many things I miss living out here. I'm afraid the boys aren't going to get as good an education in Apache Flats as they would back home."

Before Maria could comment on the statement, Seth came up to them, leading one of the horses they had brought. "Where do you want us to put these horses?" he asked.

"Oh, Diego is thrilled about the horses!" Vivienne said as she looked at the three that had been unloaded from the wagon.

"There's a corral in back of the house where you can put them. The lumber you sent arrived yesterday. It's in a wagon by the corral. Diego said that when you got here, you could help him build the stable."

"I should have known that son of mine would put me to work while I'm here," he said with a grin. "Speaking of Diego, where is he?"

"He rode out to one of the nearby ranches to investigate an attempt that had been made to kill the owner of the ranch. Hopefully, he'll be home by suppertime."

Vivienne and Maria went inside to unpack while Seth and the drivers of the coaches took care of the horses.

They had all just settled in the sitting room when they heard the boys come in the front door. "Well, our peace and quiet are over," Seth laughed as he got up and went to greet his grandsons.

"Grandpa, you're here!" Travis said excitedly as he came into the room, followed closely by Charlie Joe.

"I've missed you," the boys said giving Seth a hug before going over to Maria and hugging her.

"We've missed you too," Maria told them as Travis came and gave her a hug.

"I wish Matthew and Daniel could have come with you," Charlie Joe said. "I miss them."

"They miss you too. They wanted to come but couldn't because of school."

"Maybe they can come next summer."

"Maybe so," Maria answered. "Come into the bedroom and let me show you what we brought you."

They were happy to see their gifts but when she showed them the new game they had brought both boys faces lit up. They took the box and sat down on the floor. Travis began reading the directions on how to play Tiddley Winks. Soon they were playing the game and all else was forgotten.

"It's good to see you," Diego said to his parents when he came into the house late that evening. "I'm glad to see you made it here safe and sound. Did you have any trouble along the way?"

"No more so than those that face all travelers. Dirty hotel rooms, horses throwing shoes, excessive heat and dust and bad tempers among the travelers," Seth said as he turned his gaze to Maria.

"I believe that last complaint was directed at me," his mother said. "I'm afraid being in a small coach with your father twelve straight hours a day did cause me to lose my patience a few times. But, I think he'll forgive me."

"Just think, in a couple of weeks you can do it all over again," Diego chuckled.

"Please, don't remind me!" she said.

"We're a couple of days early, but you don't seem surprised to see us," Seth said to Diego.

"When I put my horse up I saw your coach and the horses you brought. They're all beautiful. Thank you for bringing them. I wasn't expecting more than a couple."

"I should have known you would greet the horses before you welcomed us," Seth laughed.

"You didn't expect me to walk past them and not look them over, did you?"

Seth shook his head.

"Sorry I'm so late but I was looking into an attempted murder," Diego exclaimed.

"Did you find out who it was?" his father asked.

"As a matter of fact, I did. Thanks to you and Jace. I'm finding that what works for a marshal also works for a Ranger."

"I'll have to tell your father-in-law you learned something from him while you were his deputy," Seth told him.

"Actually, I learned a lot from Jace.

"I went out to Grayson's ranch and talked with his *vaqueros*. After talking to them as a group, I sat there and studied each of them, as I had seen Jace do, until several of them started squirming in their chairs. When I didn't get any answers with that approach, I talked to each of those men individually.

"That's when I pulled your trick and started talking and asking questions non-stop," he said, looking at his father. "The third man I talked to broke down and told me it was Grayson's son-in-law who had tried to kill him.

"That's what happens when you have one of the largest ranches in the county and a young impatient son-in-law," Diego told them.

"I guess I'd better keep an eye on Cody," Seth laughed.

"I don't think you have anything to worry about where Cody's concerned. He's too grateful to you for taking him in when he was just sixteen years old, giving him a job he loves, and educating him. Not to mention, consenting to let him marry your daughter," Diego assured his father.

"I'm not sure he's always grateful to me for letting him marry Victoria," Seth laughed. "Those two still have some mighty fierce, loud arguments."

"I'm sure they always will," Diego said.

"How long did your talking spells last?" Seth asked.

"Oh, about thirty minutes for each man," Diego grinned.

"You were a good student," his father said.

"I don't think it's necessarily because he was a good student. I think, like you, talking non-stop comes natural to our son. Although, I guess, you did teach him to hone that talent to his advantage," Maria conceded.

"Well, as you can see, sometimes that trait pays off," Seth answered.

"And, sometimes, it drives your wives crazy," Maria said, looking at Vivienne and laughing.

"Did the man give you any resistance when you went to arrest him?" Maria asked.

"Very little. His wife was there and she didn't seem the least surprised or upset."

"Do you think she was in on the attempt?" Vivienne asked.

"No. I think she had found what a scoundrel her husband was and was probably glad to be rid of him."

"I hope the rest of the family wasn't too upset."

"After I brought him to the jail, I went back out to the ranch and talked to the Graysons. They both seemed rather relieved.

"Mrs. Grayson said she had always felt their daughter was a little afraid of the man. Grayson said…on second thought I don't think I'll tell you what he said about his son-in-law going to jail. I don't think you ladies would appreciate the language he used. Let's just say he had a smile on his face over the news."

"Sounds like that wasn't the first time the family has had trouble with the man," Seth said.

Chapter 7

"Since you're gone so much of the time, who's going to care for the horses we brought when you're away?" Seth asked Diego the next morning when they had all gone outside to look at the horses.

"We have a friend who has a ranch just south of here who's going to keep the stallion and brood mares on his ranch and take care of them for a fee. The two geldings I'll keep here in town. I want them to be close by in case someone is interested in buying them."

"Sounds like we're going to be building two stables," Seth said.

"No. We'll build the stable on Raul's ranch for the mares and stallion. I'll just add a couple of stalls onto the stable here at our house to keep the geldings. Vivienne said she could feed and care for the geldings when I'm not home."

"Do you mind doing that?" Seth asked Vivienne with concern.

"Not at all. The boys can help. I know they'll enjoy doing that and the responsibility will be good for them. If I have any problems or questions, we have some friends here in town who have offered to help."

"Don't let Diego overwork you," Maria told her.

"Don't worry about that, Mama. Vivienne's quite capable of saying no to me."

"My mother taught me how to say no to a husband without making him mad," Vivienne said, as she looked at Diego and smiled.

"Her mother also taught her how to put a husband in his place so he doesn't have any grounds for an argument."

"Good. Now you know what I've had to contend with since your mother and I've been married," Seth said. He looked at Maria and smiled.

"This is the first time I've seen you wear your gun in a long time," Diego said to his father.

"Things back home have become rather civilized. But I knew it was different out here and I don't want anyone to think I'm a tenderfoot."

"Are you still handy with a gun?" Diego asked. He noticed his father still wore his gun low on his hips. He remembered his mother had always told him wearing his gun low was likely to make people think he was a gunfighter.

"I'm not quite as good as I was twenty years ago, but I can still out draw and out shoot most."

"Even me?" Diego asked with a grin.

"If I can best you, I'll have my doubts about the Texas Rangers. And, before you ask, I'm not going to let you challenge me, so you can prove just how much better you are. Just remember who taught you how to handle a gun."

"Your father still doesn't like for anyone to best him at anything," his mother said with a smile. "Especially one of his own children."

"Speaking of your siblings, since Noelle's been back at the ranch, she's had me teach her how to use a gun and she's damn good."

"Sweet little Noelle?" Diego asked in surprise.

"Don't let her fool you. She can be just as spunky as that twin sister of hers. She's just not as verbal about it as Victoria.

"I think she's just waiting for Darrell to escape from prison and come after her so she can shoot him. I have no doubt, if that should happen, she'll be shooting to kill. I'm sure he knows if he comes gunning for me, I'll be shooting to kill.

And I don't miss."

"It couldn't happen to a more deserving man than Darrell," Diego said.

"Sounds like he had better stay away from Black Creek. Do you think he could possibly be released from prison before his sentence is up?" Vivienne asked.

"Not a chance. You don't plot to have the governor assassinated and get on good terms with the court system in Texas. There isn't a judge in the state who will grant him an early parole," Seth told her.

"Is Noelle still enjoying teaching?" Vivienne asked.

"Yes. Mr. Jamison says the children all adore her and try their best to please her and make her proud of them. He said he doesn't know what he would do without her. Speaking of Noelle," Maria said, "Marcus Wallace has been courting her again."

"I'm glad to hear he hasn't given up on her. It's too bad she couldn't have married Marcus in the first place instead of Darrell," Vivienne said.

"I still haven't given up that she'll eventually marry him," Maria said.

"Do you think there's a possibility of that happening?" Vivienne asked.

"I think there's a very good chance if he'll just be persistent," Maria answered.

"Matthew and Daniel miss Travis and Charlie Joe so much. They wanted so badly to come with us," Maria told her.

"I can just imagine a week in the coach with two six year old little boys," Diego said, shaking his head.

"Personally, I'd rather be stuck in the coach with those two than Selena," Seth laughed as the boys were helping them hitch the team to the wagon.

"Selena may only be seven years old but she can be quite the young lady when she needs to be," Maria said in her granddaughter's defense.

"And when she chooses not to be, she can do a fine job of displaying a temper that is equal to her mother's," Seth added.

"She only does that when she is being antagonized by her little brother and her cousin."

"I would say, in that case, she has every right to show her temper. It's her only defense against those two little rascals," Vivienne said.

"Well, son, I guess we best get this wagon full of lumber headed to that ranch so we can start building your stable," Seth said when they had the team hitched to the wagon.

"Can we go with you?" Travis asked. "Today's Saturday. We don't have to go to school."

"That's up to your mother," Seth told him.

"They can go if you and Diego promise to watch your language. And when Rafael gets there, please tell him not to tell too many wild tales. The boys still believe everything he says," Maria told him.

"We'll do our best," Diego told her.

"There should be enough food in the basket for the boy's lunches. I had a feeling they would be going with you."

"You were hoping they would go with us!" Diego said.

Vivienne just smiled.

"Yippee!" the boys exclaimed, as they jumped up and down with excitement.

"If you go with us, we're going to put you to work," Seth told them.

"Oh, boy! We're going to get to help build the stable. Papa, can I help drive the wagon?" Travis asked as he climbed onto the wagon.

"Me too!" Charlie Joe said.

"That depends on your grandpa. He's going to be doing the driving."

"We'll see about that after we get out of town," Seth told them.

"In other words, he'll say yes after they're out of our sight. Do you mind if he lets them?" Maria asked, as she and

Vivienne watched the wagon pull away from the house.

"Not at all. They're in good hands. Now, let's go inside and look closely at all the things you brought. After that, I'll show you around Apache Flats and introduce you to everyone.

"We can also go by Mr. Barnes' and take him the school books you brought and see if he can use them. He might take us to the school house and let you see inside the building. That should take care of the morning. We'll have to come up with something to do this afternoon," Vivienne laughed.

"Were the boys helpful?" Vivienne asked when they came home that evening.

"We were a lot of help," Travis told her. "We helped unload the wagon and then we held up the boards while Papa and Grandpa hammered in nails. Then we picked up all the nails they dropped."

"And they dropped a lot of nails! Grandpa gave us a penny for every nail we found. I made twenty-three cents," Charlie Joe said proudly as he pulled a handful of change out of his pocket and showed them.

"They were a lot of help and I didn't have to seriously reprimand either one of them," Diego told her.

"I'm going to go put the money I made in my room so I won't lose it," Travis said as he and Charlie Joe turned and headed for their rooms.

"After you do that go to the washroom and clean up," Vivienne called after them."

"I think one reason they behaved so well was because Papa was there. They seem to do everything they can to please him," Diego said.

"That reminds me of the only time Papa whipped me with his belt. I had said something disrespectful to Mama and that was one thing no one was allowed to do for any reason. It didn't hurt anymore than when he used his hand, but somehow it scared me more. For years after that, every time he put his hand on his belt buckle I cringed. Do you remember that?" he asked his father.

"If my memory serves me correctly, that was the last whipping I ever had to give you. And, yes, I noticed after that all I had to do was reach for my belt and you stopped whatever you were doing."

"Are you telling me you did that intentionally to scare me?"

"What do you think?" Seth asked with a grin. "That little secret kept you in line for a long time."

"Maybe you should try that on our sons," Vivienne said.

"That's a thought."

"Mama!" Travis yelled the next evening, as he came running in the kitchen door. "When I went into the chicken coop to get the eggs, there was a wolf in there! When he saw me, he growled and came running at me. If I hadn't been able to get the gate shut real fast, he would have gotten me!"

"I'll take care of him," Diego said as he and Seth came rushing into the kitchen. He grabbed the rifle from the corner near the door and they ran outside.

"Charlie Joe, you stay in here!" Maria told him, as he started to follow the men out the door.

"Oh Travis!" Vivienne said as she sat down heavily in the closest chair and drew him to her. "Are you all right?"

"Yes, ma'am. Just a little scared." As he said that, they heard a gunshot and everyone in the room jumped.

Before their nerves had calmed, Diego came back into the kitchen. "Well, the wolf is dead and I only found four dead chickens."

"I don't give a damn about the chickens!" Vivienne said, glaring at him. "We almost had a dead son!" Diego looked at Vivienne uneasily, then walked over to the corner and put the gun back where he had gotten it. "Papa and I are going to take care of the wolf and the chickens," he said as he went back out the door.

"Travis, you and Charlie Joe go to your rooms while your grandmother and I fix supper."

"But, I didn't get the eggs."

"That's all right. Your father can gather them," Vivienne told him.

"That's just one of the many things we have to contend with on a daily basis. If it's not a wolf or a rattlesnake, it's something else. I don't know how much more I can take of all the dangers the boys face," she confided to Maria, after the boys had left the room.

"I didn't realize how uncivilized things were out here. You have things happening here in town we don't even have to worry about on our ranch."

"I wish I could make Diego realize how much danger the boys are in every day. As you just saw he takes everything in stride, as though it's something everyone has to contend with.

"I guess we had best start thinking about what we're going to fix for supper," she told Maria, as she got up from her chair and slowly walked to the kitchen counter.

Maria watched as Vivienne got a bowl down from the cupboard with hands that were still trembling. *I wish there was something I could do or say to set her mind at ease, Maria thought. If I get a chance before we leave, I'm going to talk to Diego about all Vivienne has to contend with out here. I'd ask Seth to talk to him but I'm afraid he would have the same feelings about the dangers that Diego has.*

One evening when the men came in after spending the day working on the stable, Diego said, "Well, the stable is finished except for painting it. Raul said he can finish that job for us. We're going to take the horses out there tomorrow."

"Oh good," Maria said. "Now we can all have a restful visit for a few days before we have to go home."

"I'm surprised you finished it so soon," Vivienne said.

"I'm rather surprised myself. We wouldn't have been able to if we hadn't had Rafael and Raul's help. And, of course, the help of Travis and Charlie Joe. They were all good workers."

The rest of the visit was happy and the days went by too fast for everyone. Before they were ready, the day came for Seth and Maria to go home.

"I'm gonna miss you," Travis said, as they were telling them good-bye.

"We're going to miss you too. Maybe next summer all of you can come to Black Creek for a visit."

"Oh boy. Can we Mama?"

"I don't know. We'll have to see when the time gets closer."

"Thank you both for coming. We all enjoyed your visit so much," Vivienne told them. "I hope you have a safe and pleasant drive home. Be sure to write and let us know when you get there."

With a final round of hugs and kisses Seth and Maria got into the coach. Diego, Vivienne and the boys watched the coach go down the road until it was out of sight.

"I wish they could come back to Black Creek," Maria told Seth after they had been traveling for a while. "Not only do I miss them terribly, but there are so many dangers out here. Now that I've seen some of them for myself, I'm going to worry even more about them."

"They seem to be taking it all in stride," Seth said.

"You mean, Diego is taking it in stride," she said. "The boys are too young to realize how dangerous it is out here, but Vivienne is in a constant turmoil over all that could happen to them." She then proceeded to tell him some of the dangers Vivienne had told her about while they had been visiting.

"Well, there's nothing we can do about it. So try not to

worry too much," he said, as he put his arm around her and pulled her closer to him.

CHAPTER 8

A few mornings after Diego's parents left Vivienne was on her way to the General Store when she saw Lapopa walking down the street toward her. *I know a lady is suppose to cross the street or at least look the other way when they encounter a woman like Lapopa, but I'm not going to. Diego isn't here, the boys are in school and there's no one else on the street,* she thought to herself.

"Hello, Lapopa," she said with a smile when she came face to face with the woman. "I'm Vivienne Black, Diego's wife. I'm pleased to finally meet you."

Lapopa stopped and looked at her in surprise. "You know ladies like you ain't suppose to be seen talkin' to the likes of me. If somebody sees you, your reputation will be ruined," she said.

"I see nothing wrong with two women greeting each other in a friendly fashion on the street. Besides, if some old bitties look down their noses at me because I talked to you, I really don't care. I hope you have a nice day," she said as she nodded her head, then continued her walk down the street.

There's no one on the street but I'm sure someone saw me talking to Lapopa and that news will be all over town by nightfall. That thought almost made her giggle. *I know Diego won't mind that I was friendly toward her, but I suppose, I'd better tell him before someone else does.*

When Diego came home that evening and Vivienne told

him about talking to Lapopa his reaction was even better than she expected. He waited until she had finished the story then burst out laughing.

"You already knew about it didn't you?" she said.

"I stopped by the livery stable before I came home and saw Mrs. Gentry. She told me about it. You've certainly given everyone in Apache Flats something to talk about for a long time to come. I'm sure it's all over town by now what a brazen woman you are. The only woman in town who won't be appalled at what you did will be Teresa. You know your reputation is now soiled," he said before again breaking into laughter.

"How do you feel about being married to a soiled woman?"

"I like a woman who does things that aren't expected of her. You know some of the women in town are going to shun you for a while."

"Do you think it will have an adverse affect on the boys?" she asked with concern.

"No. Not in the least."

The next day when Vivienne went into the General Store and Teresa saw her she broke into laughter. "You know you're the talk of the town," she said. "Even I haven't had the nerve to do more than simply nod in passing at the woman. Mrs. Gentry was in here earlier and was appalled that you would do such a thing. Everyone else I've talked to thought it was funny. Several said they wished they had the nerve to do what you did.

"What did Diego have to say when you told him?"

"I thought he would never stop laughing. He did say some of the ladies would probably shun me for a while."

"I don't think anyone will do that except Mrs. Gentry."

"She already does that. Apparently she thinks the wife of a Texas Ranger isn't worthy of her friendship. I wonder how she would feel if she knew Diego's family owns one of the largest and most respectable ranches in Bexar County?"

"Why don't you tell her and find out?"

"No thank you. I like our relationship just the way it is. I have no desire to be her friend. She's one of the few people I've ever known who I don't care for."

When Diego came back to the house, shortly after leaving, Vivienne knew something was wrong.

"I just got a telegram from Captain Jones that two cattle barons east of here are in the midst of a range war. I'm fixin' to go to Ft. Stockton to meet him and Sergeant Kelton. We're going to talk to the ranchers and try to settle this thing peacefully," he said.

"Are you leaving now?" she asked.

"As soon as I get my gear together."

"While you're doing that, I'll fix you something to eat. Do you have any idea how long you'll be gone?"

"At least a week," he said as he went into the bedroom to get a change of clothes.

"Oh. That long?" she managed to say, stunned. "I'll pack some food for you to take with you."

After putting his bedroll, several extra rounds of ammunition for his rifle and six shooter and some other things he would need for a week on the trail on the back of a pack horse, he came back into the kitchen.

"Please be careful," Vivienne said when he sat down at the table to eat.

"I promise I will. I wish I could tell the boys good-bye but I've got to leave before they come home for lunch."

"I'll tell them good-bye for you and give them your love."

"Thank you. I love you," he said as he got up from the table and took her in his arms and held her.

"I love you too," she said. His lips met hers and they kissed.

"Hmm, I do have time to give you a proper good-bye," he said before giving her another long, passionate kiss. Still kissing her, he picked her up, carried her into the bedroom and put her on the bed.

"Oh, that was good," Vivienne said, snuggling up to him after they made love.

"It's always good with you. I guess I'd better go now," he said reluctantly, as he slowly got out of bed and began dressing. After another long kiss he was out the door and on his way to Ft. Stockton.

The next evening, when Diego reached the old fort, Captain Jones was there waiting for him.

"Howdy, Lieutenant," the captain said, as they shook hands. "I didn't expect you until at least tomorrow. You had farther to come than either Sergeant Kelton or myself."

"Good horses. Besides being a Ranger, I'm also in the horse breeding business. I have several for sale that I can let you have for a good price, in case you're interested."

"It sounds like I'll have to make a trip to Apache Flats sometime in the near future and take a look at those horses of yours," the captain said after Diego told him about the two geldings he had.

"Ole' Red here has served me well, but the years have slowed him down and he's not quite as alert as he use to be," the captain added as he gave the horse a pat on the shoulder.

"Papa just brought the horses to me last month, so I haven't had a chance to ride either of them very much, but I think the bay would be a good mount for you. He's fast and has a calm disposition."

"In that case, keep him for me and I'll buy him the next time I make it to Apache Flats."

"Thanks. I'll do that," Diego told him.

"The first thing we're going to do when we get to Saint Gaul is find out from Sheriff Larson what he can tell us about what's going on between the two ranches. Then we'll go out to the ranches and see what we can do about the problem.

"It's hard for me to believe the area I first saw as dry, open ranch land, that would only support a few head of sheep, is now irrigated farm land," the captain said thoughtfully, as he looked over the fields as they rode to town.

"How did the transformation come to be?" Diego asked.

"About ten years ago some enterprising young men from San Antonio thought Comanche Springs would be a good source of water to irrigate the area and grow grains. So, they bought the land and did just that. To the surprise of a lot of people, it's been a very successful and prosperous venture."

"Isn't there a problem between the farmers and ranchers?" Diego asked.

"You'd think there would be, but the ranchers know they need the grain to feed their stock in the winter and the farmers know their livelihood comes from the ranchers. So, for the most part, they get along rather peacefully.

"This is another of west Texas' large towns," the captain laughed, as they rode down the one street of Saint Gaul to the sheriff's office.

"Good evening, Sheriff Larson," Captain Jones said as they went into the sheriff's office. "This is one of my Ranger partners, Lieutenant Black. Sergeant Kelton will be joining us tomorrow."

"Nice to meet you, Lieutenant Black. Thank you both for comin'," the sheriff said as he and Diego shook hands.

"It's good to meet you, Sheriff. I'm glad we were available to come help you," Diego answered.

"You want to tell us what we'll be up against when we get out to the ranches?" the captain asked.

"Well, it hasn't developed into a full-fledged range war yet, and I want to stop it before it does. That's why I asked for your help. Each of the ranchers is accusing the other of rustling their cattle. There's only been random shooting so far. Nobody's been killed and I want to keep it that way. Me and my deputy have looked around both ranches and talked to several of the cowboys. We can't seem to get to the bottom of the situation. I'm hoping you can."

Sergeant Kelton arrived the next morning. After briefing him on the situation, the three men headed out to confront the feuding ranchers.

As they rode, Captain Jones told them his plans for solving the problem. "I know you're both excellent shots," he said, looking at each of them in turn, "but, if there's any shooting involved, I want you to remember these are ranchers we're dealing with, not outlaws. Don't shoot to kill."

"Yes sir," they both answered respectfully.

Just as they brought their horses to a stop in front of a large two storied, frame house, a man walked out the door onto the porch. "We're looking for Howard Bickford," the captain announced.

"He's inside," the man said abruptly, pointing his thumb toward the door. Without looking at them he walked down the steps to where his horse was tied. Mounting, he rode off.

"You get the feeling he's not pleased to see us?" Sergeant Kelton asked quietly.

Diego didn't say anything, but he imagined they would get the same response from Bickford.

As they dismounted, the front door opened again and a middle aged man of average height with thinning gray hair walked out onto the porch. "You lookin' fer me? I'm Howard Bickford."

"Yes sir," Captain Jones said. "We heard there was some trouble between your ranch and the Triple Q."

"You musta' heard wrong. Me and Quist ain't never been on better terms," Bickford told him.

"That's strange. We got our information from a very reliable source."

"Well, sometimes even reliable sources can be wrong. I'm sure Quist'll tell ya' the same thing I just told ya'," Bickford said.

"I'm glad to hear that. Be sure it stays that way or we'll be back," the captain said, as the three Rangers remounted their horses and turned them away from the house.

"It seems word got to the ranchers the Rangers were coming and they don't want to deal with us," Sergeant Kelton said as they rode toward the Triple Q.

"You'd be surprised how often that happens. I'm sure, if there is a truce, it will only last until we're out of the area," Captain Jones told him.

"What are we going to do now?" Sergeant Kelton asked.

"First, we're fixin' to find out what the Triple Q men have to say about the situation."

"If they tell us the same thing Bickford did, what are we going to do?" Diego asked.

"We won't have any choice but to ride on. I'll stick around for a few days and see if things stay settled."

When they got to the Triple Q and talked to Quist, he too acted surprised to see the Rangers and to hear there was trouble between the two ranches.

After the captain told Quist the same thing he had told Bickford, the three Rangers turned their horses and headed back to town to tell Sheriff Larson what the two ranchers had said.

"Sorry ya'll had to be bothered with coming all this way," the captain told Diego and Sergeant Kelton.

"It was quite obvious they were both lying," Diego said. "Things are bound to get back to the way they were shortly. Feuding ranchers can only stay on friendly terms for so long. Captain, for the time being, things are quiet around Apache Flats. I'll stay here with you for a while." "How about you, Sergeant Kelton?" the captain asked.

"We're short of lawmen in my territory. I'd rather not be gone too long. Since we don't know if, or when, there's going to be another outbreak of trouble here, would it be all right if I go back to my territory now?" Sergeant Kelton asked.

"That's fine. There's a chance nothing more will happen. There's no sense sticking around here when you're needed more at home. The sheriff, Diego and I should be able to handle the situation here."

"Thank you, sir," the sergeant said.

"Those lying bastards!" Sheriff Larson said when they got back to Saint Gaul and told him what the two men had said.

"Lieutenant Black and I are going to camp outside of town for a few days. On my way into town yesterday I saw a draw a couple of miles north of here where we can stay without anyone knowing we're here. If they should start their gunplay again, let us know."

"Thanks. I'll do that," the sheriff told them.

"Well, Lieutenant, it looks like it's gonna' be just the two of us for a few days," Captain Jones told Diego as they were making camp. "Let's hope we come out of this still on friendly terms.

"How does your wife like living in Apache Flats?"

"She's all right with it. I know she misses our families, but she's made friends in Apache Flats and seems to be happy there. She grew up in a small town about a hundred miles west of here so she knew what life was going to be like before we moved there."

"How did the two of you meet?"

"We were both students at Salado College. She was a freshman and I was a senior. After I graduated and went back to the ranch, I realized I was in love with her and wanted to marry her.

"The funny thing was when our fathers met they looked so much alike it was uncanny. They look enough alike to be twins. They started talking and discovered they're half cousins no one knew about."

"Small world. I met my wife when I was working the border in the Rio Grande Valley. The evening we met it only took me a few minutes to be captivated by her. I knew that very night she was the woman I wanted to spend the rest of my life with. However, I'll admit, it took me a while to convince her she wanted to spend her life married to a Ranger.

"Well, Lieutenant, it's about time for supper," the captain said, as he looked at the western horizon and saw the sun was setting. "Which one of us is going to be the cook?"

"As you know from the time you came to Apache Flats and I fixed lunch for us, cooking is not one of my strong points. My family has voted my father the world's worst cook and I've been told I run him a close second. I think for both our sakes, I'd best let you do the cooking and I'll do the cleaning up," Diego laughed.

"We'll have to make do with a small campfire. We don't want our whereabouts to be discovered because of the smoke. So, do you want beans or beans?" the captain asked.

"I believe I'll have beans."

CHAPTER 9

The second afternoon they were in the draw, the sheriff came to tell them the range war had started back up.

When they returned to town, the deputy sheriff and two more, newly deputized, men joined them and they rode out to the Triple Q.

They had just gotten onto the ranch when they were met by Quist and a dozen of his cowboys.

"A herd of my cattle was stolen last night," he told the lawmen. "We followed the tracks an' they led to a draw that heads to Bickford's ranch. When we got into the draw, we was ambushed by Bickford's men. We're going there now an' have a showdown with them thieving bastards."

"Hold it right there," Captain Jones said, as the men again started toward Bickford's ranch. "The six of us will handle the situation."

"Like hell, ya' will. I'm tired of waitin' fer the law to do anything. We're taking care of the problem once an' fer all," he said, looking angrily at the captain.

"No. You aren't," the captain said calmly, but firmly. His eyes and those of Diego's never left the men as the two Rangers slowly drew their guns.

"There's only six of you an' there's a dozen of us," Quist snarled. "Ya' can't stop us."

"The only way you're getting past us is to kill us and I don't think you want to kill a sheriff and two Texas Rangers," Captain Jones said.

"Go on back to your ranch–Now!"

The two groups of men glared silently at each other for several seconds until Quist finally said, "At least let us show you where the tracks were headed when we was ambushed."

"That we'll do."

After they took the lawmen to the draw, Quist and his men reluctantly headed back to their ranch headquarters.

"Before we do anything else, we're going to Bickford's ranch and talk to him," the captain explained.

"What good will talking do if he's stealing Quist's cattle?" the sheriff asked. "We'll just be met by flying lead like Quist's men were!"

"I don't think so. Just follow me. I have a gut feeling about this," Captain Jones said, as he turned his horse toward the Bickford ranch.

They hadn't ridden far when they were met by Bickford and four of his men. "We're going after that cattle rustling son-of-a-bitch Quist an' ya' can't stop us," Bickford said when the two groups of men were facing each other.

"Before you do that, tell us what happened," Captain Jones said.

Bickford then began telling them the same story they had just heard from Quist. Bickford's men had been trailing their cattle that were headed toward Quist's ranch when they had been ambushed in the draw. This time the supposed rustlers and ambushers were Quist and his men.

"Go on back home and let us handle this."

"What makes ya' think the six of ya'll can handle this. There's about a dozen of Quist's men waiting in that draw to ambush ya'," Bickford said.

"Don't worry about us. We can handle the situation and you'll have your cattle back by the end of the day."

"Ranger, yer crazy," Bickford said.

"Maybe," the captain said. "Just do as I told you. If you take the law into your own hands, you'll end up in jail or, more likely, at the end of a rope. I don't think you want either of those things to happen."

"All right. We'll give ya'll 'til the end of the day; then we're goin' after Quist." With those words he turned his horse in the direction they had come from and signaled his men to follow.

"Now," Captain Jones said, as they watched the men ride off, "let's go to that draw and get those cattle."

They followed the tracks of the herd until they disappeared into the rocks of the dry creek bed. As they continued down the draw, it widened and the sides became higher and steeper until they found themselves in a canyon.

Captain Jones was silent as he rode slowly, looking at the sides of the canyon.

"What are we looking for?" the sheriff asked. "I can tell ya' there's no trail up the side of this canyon. The walls are too steep."

"I'm not sure what I'm looking for, but I'll know when I see it. I found out a long time ago, you don't look for evidence. You look for the things that added together make the evidence," he said thoughtfully, without his eyes ever leaving the sides of the canyon.

They hadn't ridden much farther when the captain suddenly reined in his horse and sat studying the west wall of the canyon.

"Do you notice anything unusual about that spot?" he asked Diego, indicating the area he was looking at.

"Well, the side is covered with rocks and heavy brush," Diego said thoughtfully, as he looked carefully at the side of the canyon. "All the brush is green and thick, except for the section there where everything's dead," he said pointing to a spot on the canyon wall.

The captain got off his horse and walked over to the wall. He ran his hand across it and began pulling the dead bushes away and tossing them aside. Before long, where the dead brush had been, they saw two large rocks leaning against the side of the canyon. Rocks that didn't match the others around them.

"Come help me move these rocks," the captain said.

After several minutes of hard pushing, the men managed to move one of the rocks aside. Behind where the rock had been they found a cave.

"Well, I'll be damned! I bet I've been down this canyon a hundred times and I ain't never seen this," Sheriff Larson said.

"That's because you weren't looking for something that wasn't right," Captain Jones told him.

"I'll be willing to bet there's another opening to this cave somewhere on the other side of the canyon," the captain said, walking inside.

"Do you think this is the passage the rustlers are using to get the cattle off the ranches?" Diego asked.

"That's my guess."

As his eyes adjusted to the darkness in the cave, Diego saw the fresh tracks of cattle and their droppings. "I'll be damned," he said quietly, as he looked at the tracks. "Now all we have to do is find the other entrance and we'll find those cattle. I think it's best we get out of here. I don't want to find ourselves trapped in here," the captain said. "We'll have to find the other entrance while we're above ground. It's probably as well concealed as this one was. It will take longer to find that way, but it'll be a hell of a lot safer."

"There's a narrow passage a couple of miles ahead that'll take us to the other side of the canyon," the sheriff told them.

As they had expected, the ride around the canyon was long and tedious. It took quite a while to find the other opening to the cave, but once found, it was only a short time until they found the tracks of a large herd of cattle being driven west.

"Well, Lieutenant, can you tell about how many cattle there are, how many men are driving them, and how old the tracks are?" the captain asked Diego.

"You don't ask for much!" Diego said as he studied the tracks.

"I've been told you're the best tracker in the state. Now,

you can either prove that to be a fact or just another rumor," he said, grinning.

After following the tracks and studying them for several minutes, Diego came back with a report. "There are approximately six *vaqueros*, a hundred head of cattle and the tracks were made early this morning. They're covered with dried dew."

"Sheriff, I think you, the lieutenant and I can handle six men. You can send your deputies back to tell Quist and Bickford we've found the rustlers tracks, but we may not have them in hand until late tonight. You might also tell them come morning they can come round up their cattle."

When they got away from the rocks of the canyon and on the dry, soft dirt, the tracks were easier to follow. They rode fast for the first couple of hours to make up for the lead the rustlers had on them.

Just before sundown, they slowed down so Diego could study the tracks more closely. "The herd is about an hour ahead of us," he told them.

"Good. We'll go on the other side of those hills just ahead and use them as cover from the rustlers," the captain told them. "I'm certain they'll be staying to the low ground."

"They probably will. However, won't they most likely have a scout riding the high ground who will spot us?" Diego asked.

"That's a possibility but, hopefully, they won't want to take one of their men away from the herd to do that. I imagine, at this time, getting the cattle away from here as fast as they can is their utmost concern. Anyway, that's a chance we'll have to take. Come dark, after they've made camp for the night, we'll make our move on 'em."

When they got close enough to hear the lowing of the cattle, they tied their horses to some trees and walked slowly and quietly up the hill. Just before reaching the crest of the hill, the men lowered themselves and crawled the rest of the way so they wouldn't be seen or heard.

As they silently looked down at the herd, they saw the

cattle were settled down for the night and the men were gathered around the campfire eating.

"It doesn't look like they've posted any men around the cattle. So, it will be easy enough to surround them," the captain said quietly.

"Sheriff, I want you to go to that clump of trees on the east side of the campfire. Lieutenant, make your way to that large rock on the south side. I'll come up from behind the horses. That way we'll be on three sides of them and the cattle will be on the fourth side. Come dark, we'll make our move," the captain told them. They walked back down the hill to where their horses were tied.

"I think it's dark enough now that we can manage to surround those rustlers without them seeing us," the captain said a little later. "Wait for my signal before you make your move and watch out for those cattle. When the shooting starts, they'll more than likely stampede."

The three lawmen quietly headed for the spots they had been assigned. Diego noticed the captain had sent the sheriff to the most protected of the three spots and he had taken the most open and dangerous position for himself.

Diego had only been behind the rock a couple of minutes and had quietly cocked his rifle when he heard Captain Jones shout, "Texas Rangers. Put your hands up."

As they had known would happen, the rustlers didn't do as the captain ordered. Suddenly, the silence was broken by the sound of gunfire being exchanged between the rustlers and lawmen and the cattle stampeding.

The lawmen had the advantage in the gunfight. Not only were the rustlers in the open, without any protection, the light from the campfire made them easy targets. In just a matter of minutes there were five rustlers lying on the ground, either dead or wounded. The only sound was that of the cattle running from the sound of the gunfire.

With their guns reloaded and pointed at the rustlers, the three lawmen came from behind their cover and walked toward the campfire. Silently they disarmed the three surviving rustlers and tied their hands behind their backs. then they threw the two dead rustlers across the backs of a couple of horses.

"Lieutenant, if you and the sheriff will keep an eye on these *hombres*, I'll go get our horses. Remember what I said earlier about shooting to kill," he said, winking at Diego inconspicuously.

"The three of you might like to know when my partner here shoots at someone, he doesn't miss and he doesn't aim for an arm or a leg." With those words, the captain walked into the darkness to get the horses.

"Well, Lieutenant," Captain Jones said when he returned, "you said there were about six rustlers and a hundred head of cattle. There were five rustlers and from what I could tell you weren't far off on how many cattle there were either. In the morning after the ranchers round up the cattle, we'll see just how close you were. You just may be the best tracker in the state after all."

"Thank you sir," Diego replied.

"These rustlers were pretty crafty," the captain said. "They had the ranchers so busy accusing each other of the rustling they didn't have time to think there might be someone else who was stealing their cattle."

After going to the two ranch headquarters to tell the ranchers the rustlers had been caught and where their cattle could be found, they took the rustlers to town. While the sheriff took the three surviving rustlers to the jail, Diego and the captain took the two dead men to the undertaker.

"I think after finding his stolen cattle and preventing a range war, the least Bickford can do is put us up for the night in that big house of his," Captain Jones said with a grin. With that, the two Rangers turned their horses toward Bickford's ranch.

"I'm glad none of the rustlers were from either of the ranches. Hopefully, after both of the ranchers eat a little crow they'll become friends again," Diego said.

The next morning after spending the night at Bickford's and another gracious thank you from the ranchers and the sheriff, the captain and Diego headed for home.

CHAPTER 10

"You're home!" Vivienne cried as Diego came in the house a few days later. "I didn't hear you ride up. I've missed you so much."

"I came around to the back of the house because I wanted to surprise you. I've missed you too. She went into his arms and he kissed her hungrily.

"It's still a couple of hours before the boys get home from school," he said, as he looked across the room at the clock. "As soon as I get cleaned up we're going to the bedroom and celebrate my homecoming properly."

"Is that all you ever think about?"

"No. Sometimes I think about eating and sometimes I just think about you," he teased, smiling.

"Well, I'm glad to know I'm on your list somewhere," she said returning his smile.

"I noticed when I put my horse up the sorrel wasn't in his stall. Did you sell him?" Diego asked hopefully, as she was putting water on the stove to heat for his bath.

"Yes."

"Who bought him?"

"Rafael."

"Oh! I hope you didn't let him talk you into letting him have the horse for too low a price," he said with concern. He knew what a smooth talker Rafael could be, especially with the ladies.

"Don't worry, I didn't. But it wasn't because he didn't try. He started by telling me how beautiful I am and what a good cook I am and what a good mother I am and ended with what a tough *hombre* I am to do business with," she chuckled. "I did come down a tiny bit from the price you told me, to soothe his pride for having to do business with a woman."

"That's fine. The price I told you was more than I expected to get. I should have known that's the horse that would catch Rafael's eye. He was the showiest of the two geldings.

"Most likely he intentionally waited until I was out of town, thinking, because you're a woman, he could charm you into letting him have the horse for a lower price than I would.

"Since that ploy failed I'm surprised he didn't try something else to make you come down more on the price. He must have really wanted the horse."

"He's so proud of that horse. He rides him everywhere. I don't think he walks anywhere anymore. Oh, he named him El Conquistador."

"That figures! A showy name for the showy horse of a showy man." Diego laughed.

"You know, everything he said about you is true."

"Even about me being a tough *hombre* to do business with?" she asked.

"Yes. You can be a tough *hombre* when you need to be. If you don't believe me, just ask Travis and Charlie Joe.

"Do I have reason to be jealous of Rafael?" he teased.

"Not hardly. I like to be the only woman in a man's life. I think half the women in the area have been involved with Rafael at one time or another, and I imagine half of those women are still in love with him."

"You'll always be the one and only for me," Diego said. He drew her close and kissed her again.

"Captain Jones is going to buy the bay gelding. The sale of those two horses will pay the year's rent, that we need to pay Raul to look after the mares. Now all we have to do is wait until the foals which are due next spring, to get old enough to sell. Then we can start making a profit on the horses.

"I'd better go get that bath before the water gets cold."

"And a shave," she added.

"I thought I'd keep this," he said running his hand across his beard.

"Fine. That's up to you. But, if you do, I'll tell you now, I'm leaving, and you'll not only have your beard but two little boys to keep you company," she teased.

"Where's my razor?" he asked as he went into the washroom.

"Now, let's get down to serious business," Diego said when he came back into the kitchen after bathing and shaving, with only a towel wrapped around his waist.

"You look and smell so much better now," Vivienne cooed as they kissed. "The boys will be home in about an hour."

"Don't worry. This won't take long. I've been thinking about this since I walked in the door and saw you," he said. As he picked her up the towel around his waist fell to the floor.

They had just gotten out of bed and were dressing when they heard the boys come in the house. "That was close," Diego said quietly as he let out a deep sigh of relief and ran a comb through his hair "How would we have ever explained to them why we were in bed in the middle of the day?"

"If you don't wipe that big smile off your face before you see them, you're going to have to explain that to them anyway," she told him.

"Charlie Joe convinces me more every day he's just like you. Yesterday, when Teresa and Paco were here, I overheard him tell Paco that he's not scared of anything," Vivienne told him that evening.

"You didn't believe him?" Diego asked.

"Oh, I believed him. He's proven that to me on numerous occasions.

"This morning, before the boys went to school, we were

outside when a huge rattlesnake went slithering across the yard. Charlie Joe ran to get the hoe and would have tried to kill the snake himself if I hadn't grabbed the hoe from him and done it. I had a terrible time convincing him he wasn't strong enough to be able to hit it with enough force to kill it. He would have only made it mad and it would have bitten him. I'm afraid one of these days I'm not going to be around and he's going to try it. That's just one of the things I'm constantly worrying about."

Diego looked at her questioningly.

"Your mother told me, when you were about Charlie Joe's age, you told her you weren't scared of anything. How much has changed since then?"

"Well, now that you mention it, I'll have to admit, very little."

"That what I thought."

A few days later when Diego came home for the night Vivienne handed him a letter from Captain Jones.

"Interesting," he said as he read the letter. "The captain says the three rustlers we caught last week were also wanted for robbery and murder. He's almost certain when they go to trial they'll be sentenced to hang. He said when I studied the tracks of the rustled cattle and told him there were about one hundred head my estimate was even closer than he had predicted. He got a letter from Sheriff Larson telling him the ranchers found ninety-three head. He said, in his eyes, I have now become the best tracker in the state."

"Congratulations!"

"Thanks. But remember, that's just the opinion of one man."

"Yes. But that's not the opinion of just any man. That's the opinion of Captain T. P. Jones."

"Careful, dear. My head's liable to get even bigger than it already is."

"That's impossible," she laughed.

"Next time I see the captain I'll have to tell him you have put him a step above the average man.

"He also said to be on the lookout for some disgruntled Indians who tried to kidnap a young girl south of here," he said thoughtfully as he read the rest of the letter.

"I can't tell you how pleased I am that Paco and Charlie Joe have become such good friends," Teresa said one afternoon, as she and Vivienne sat in back of the General Store watching the boys play Tiddley Winks. "He becomes bored so easily. I was hoping after he started to school he wouldn't get bored so often. But it hasn't seemed to help."

"I know. I was hoping the same thing about Charlie Joe. But it seems all it's done is give him something to complain about." They watched the boys playing their game until Paco flipped his last wink into the cup and won the game.

"Charlie Joe Black, come here this instant!"

At his mother's words he immediately jumped up and went to where she was sitting.

"What did I hear you just say?" she asked.

"I said, oh hell," he said quietly, as he dropped his head and looked at the ground.

"You know you're not suppose to say that word. The next time I hear you say it, you will be punished."

"Yes, ma'am. But Papa says it."

"I don't care who says it, you and your brother do not ever use that word. Is that clear?"

"Yes ma'am."

"Good. Now go back to your game before I change my mind and decide to punish you this time."

At that he turned and ran back to where Paco was waiting for him.

"He certainly came quickly and listened well," Teresa said.

"Both boys know when I use their full name they're in serious trouble and had better do what they're told. I also think he was rather embarrassed to be chastised in front of

Paco. If you noticed, even at that, he had an excuse for using the word.

"I'm going to have to, once again, remind Diego not to use certain words around the boys. They both seem to enjoy repeating words they know they're not suppose to say."

"Good luck," Teresa told her. "I can't tell you how many times I've reminded Joaquin about that very thing. He's very careful how he talks around Evita and Juana, but he seems to think it's all right to use bad words around Paco. I think he believes it will make a man of Paco if he uses those words."

"Neither of you boys are eating your peas," Vivienne said that evening at supper, as she looked at Travis and Charlie Joe's plates.

"Do we have to?" Charlie Joe whined. "They taste awful."

"You know the rules. You have to eat three bites which is all I put on your plates. If you want to grow up to be big and strong, like your papa, you have to eat your vegetables."

"I eat my peas with honey. I've done it all my life. It makes the peas taste funny but it keeps them on my knife," Diego said with a grin.

At that the boys smiled and looked hopefully at their mother.

"Before the two of you ask, no, you may not eat your peas or anything else that way," Vivienne told them when she saw the hopeful expressions on their faces.

"And you, Mr. Black, can keep your witticisms to yourself. I'm sure your mother never let you eat your peas that way," she said. She turned and gave Diego a warning look.

"I guess I'd better be quiet."

"I think that's an excellent idea."

"I bet they'd be good that way," Charlie Joe said, as he took a bite of peas and made a face.

"Son, I'd advise you to keep quiet also, unless you want your mother's wrath to come down on you," Diego said, suppressing a grin.

"That's very good advice," Vivienne said, staring at the three of them.

The next morning, when they went to the meeting hall to hear the traveling minister, Vivienne noticed there were more Indians than usual standing around the building, waiting to go inside. Generally that didn't bother her, but this morning two of the men she had not seen before were watching the children in a way that made her very uneasy.

Even now, after the Indian wars were over for the most part, she knew many of them still felt resentment toward the white people, because their land had been taken away from them. To make matters worse, many Indians had died as a result of small pox and other diseases the white man had brought with them that they had no immunity to. She couldn't say she blamed them for their resentment, but when there were so many of them around she always felt rather nervous. She drew the boys close to her and walked a little closer to Diego.

As she moved closer to him, he put his arm around her and watched the two men closely. Her uneasiness with the Indians was one of the few things about the area she and Diego were in agreement about.

CHAPTER 11

The family had spent the day visiting the Hildalgos and checking on the mares. "It looks like both the bays will be dropping their foals in the next couple of weeks. The gray probably won't be dropping hers for at least another month," Diego told Vivienne on the way back to Apache Flats that evening.

"Are you going to be breeding the mares again this spring?" she asked.

"All but the gray. She's too young to have another foal so soon after this one. I'm going to wait until next year to breed her again.

"I'm surprised how many people have bred their mares to the stallion. Thanks to that, financially, we're managing to break even on the horses. Hopefully, next year, after selling the foals that are born this spring, we'll start seeing some profit."

The boys had had a full, busy day, leaving them tired, cranky and irritable. Ever since leaving the Hidalgos' they had been arguing about one thing or another. Vivienne had told them several times to stop, but her words were only obeyed for a few minutes, then the arguing started up again. Suddenly, Diego reined the horse in and brought the buggy to an abrupt stop. Turning around, he looked sternly at the boys. "Travis, Charlie Joe, if the two of you don't stop arguing right now, I'm going to make you get out of the buggy and walk the rest of the way home." His tone of voice was low and firm, leaving no doubt in their minds they had better do what he had suggested.

"Papa, you can't do that! It's getting dark and there are rattlesnakes and wolves and wild Indians out there. And Charlie Joe would be scared." The longer he talked and thought about walking home, the bigger his eyes got.

"I wouldn't be scared!" Charlie Joe said in his defense.

"Does that mean you want to walk home?" Diego asked.

"No."

"No, what?" Diego asked.

"No, sir. But, if I did, I wouldn't be scared."

"Since neither of you want to walk, I advise you to stop arguing," Diego told them.

After a solemn "Yes, sir" from both boys, Diego flicked the reins and the horse started up again.

When there had been no bickering for several minutes Vivienne turned and saw both boys were asleep. "You really knew how to stop their bickering," she said quietly.

"Papa used that threat on Antonio and me when we were youngsters and it always worked. I hope it continues to work on our two little rascals as well.

"Charlie Joe's braver than I am. I'd be scared to walk that distance without a gun," Diego said under his breath.

"Would you really have made them walk all the way home?" Vivienne whispered.

"No. But don't tell them that," he whispered back.

"I'm surprised neither you or Antonio called your father on that threat."

"Papa didn't make idle threats. We all found that out the hard way, at an early age. To this day I'm convinced, we would have found ourselves walking if we hadn't stopped arguing."

"You don't think your mother would have protested?"

"No. She could be just as tough as Papa when it came to disciplining us."

"I guess she had to be with five children and two of them were you and Antonio. It's amazing how the boys pay more attention to your threats than they do mine."

"That's because, like my papa, they both know I don't make idle threats. And, I whip harder than you do," he grinned.

"Are you implying I make idle threats?"

"Never," he said. "You can be just as tough as my mother could be."

The rest of the trip was spent in silence.

As winter progressed, the weather grew colder and windier. It was the coldest weather any of them had ever experienced.

"I never thought a little snow would send you back home," Vivienne said when Diego came into the house, just minutes after leaving one cold February morning.

"A little snow wouldn't, but I think a bad storm is headed this way. The western sky is the darkest, most eerie shade of blue I've ever seen. I've heard about what can happen to people caught out in a blizzard. I have no desire to freeze to death."

"I wonder if Mr. Barnes is going to let school out early because of the storm? I hope the boys make it home safely before it hits," Vivienne said as she looked worriedly out the window.

About that time the front door came flying open and the boys ran into the room.

"It's snowing! Mr. Barnes said there's a blizzard coming and he let us come home. He said we don't have to go back to school until it's over! What's a blizzard?" Charlie Joe asked.

"Oh, Charlie Joe, didn't you listen to anything Mr. Barnes said?" Travis asked. He looked at his little brother with disgust.

"Of course I did. He said there's a blizzard headed this way and we don't have to go back to school until it's over."

"A blizzard is when the wind is blowing hard, and the snow is coming down so fast and furious you can't see more than a couple of feet in front of you," Vivienne told him.

"What about the children who don't live within walking distance of the school?" she asked.

"Mr. Barnes said he would take them home," Travis told her.

"Great! Not only am I trapped inside all day, but both boys will be cooped up in here with me," Diego said with a quiet groan.

"Quit your complaining and go build a fire in the fireplace, while I fix some hot chocolate and coffee."

As the day progressed, the temperature continued to drop and the wind increased. By early evening the predicted storm was blowing in full force.

They had finished supper and were gathered around the fireplace. Diego had found a book he hadn't had time to finish reading while Vivienne sat on the floor playing Tiddly Winks with the boys. Suddenly, there was a knock at the back door.

"What fool would be out in this weather?" Diego asked. He got up and went to answer the door.

"It must be someone we know well. No one ever comes to the back door," Vivienne said.

"Captain Jones! What are you doing out in this weather?" Diego asked, surprised when he saw who was there.

"Believe me, it's not by choice," the captain said. He took off his gloves and rubbed his hands together. "I was on my way back to San Angelo and thought I'd swing by here and get that horse you have for me, when this blizzard hit. I was hoping to make it here before getting caught out in the middle of it but I didn't quite make it.

"Do you mind an unexpected overnight guest?" he asked Vivienne when she came into the kitchen.

"Of course not. You're always welcome in our home. Please feel free to stay until the weather clears. I just made a fresh pot of coffee. I'll heat up something for you to eat as well."

"Thank you, ma'am. I don't want to put you out, but I

sure would appreciate that."

"Oh, hi Captain Jones," Charlie Joe said when he and Travis came into the kitchen to see who was there. "Papa said he wondered what fool would be out in this weather." Suddenly, it got very quiet. Looking around the room, Charlie Joe saw everyone, including his brother, was looking at him. "I shouldn't have said that, should I?"

"No you shouldn't have," his mother answered.

"I'm sorry," he said, as he tucked his head and looked at the floor.

"Your apology is accepted," the captain said. He then burst out laughing.

"While you wrap your hands around a cup of hot coffee and warm up, I'll go tend to your horse," Diego said.

"Thank you, but I've already done that. I knew you wouldn't turn a foolish old man away from your door in weather like this," the captain said with a grin.

"If you hadn't been home, I planned to sleep in the stall with my horse. But, I'll admit, a nice soft bed in a warm house is more inviting than a bed of hay in a cold barn."

The fierce storm raged throughout the night. The wind howled, rattling the windows and, at one point, blew the front door open. By breakfast the next morning the wind had died down but there was still a light snow falling and the ground was covered with over a foot of soft snow.

"After breakfast we'll go outside and build a snowman," Diego told the boys.

"What's a snowman?" Travis asked.

"You're about to find out. Snow doesn't come very often in the San Antonio area, but the one time it did I was about your age. We barely had enough snow to build a snowman but I think I still remember how to do it."

"Can I help?" the captain asked.

They all turned and looked at him in surprise. "By all means! After Vivienne gets the boys bundled up to her satisfaction, we'll go out there and build the best snowman this town has ever seen."

Vivienne remained in the warm kitchen, washing the breakfast dishes and looking out the window, watching the snowman being built. She smiled as she noticed the two men were enjoying themselves as much as the boys.

The snowman was almost finished when she saw Charlie Joe step away and go over to the side of the house where there was a deep snowdrift. He grabbed a handful of snow, rolled it into a ball like his father had showed him and threw it at his father. His aim was a little off. The snowball missed Diego and hit Captain Jones in the back.

Since the captain had his back to her, Vivienne couldn't see his face when the snowball hit him. She did notice his hand automatically went to his hip where his gun usually rested. The terrified look on Charlie Joe's face when he saw who his snowball had hit brought a smile to her face. She was certain the captain would also take this offense in good humor.

Sure enough, the captain slowly turned around and, with a smile on his face, drew his arm back and threw a snowball at Charlie Joe. His snowball didn't miss it's target. Suddenly, the snowman was forgotten and a full-fledged snowball fight was in progress.

Later that day, when it had stopped snowing and the weather had warmed up, Diego and the captain went out to the Hidalgo's to get the captain's horse.

"Well, how do you like him?" Diego asked on the ride back to town.

"He's everything you said he would be. I think we're going to make a good team. As soon as the ground dries out a bit I'm going to see if he's as fast as you say he is."

"I see the boys finished the snowman while we were gone," Diego said as they rode up to the house. "I wonder if Vivienne helped them?"

"If she was smart she stayed inside and watched. I hope that hat they put on him was one you weren't planning to wear again."

"My sweet little wife knows how to get her way. She's been trying to get me to get rid of that hat for months. Now, it looks like I won't have any choice but to do that," Diego laughed.

"It's been a good day," Diego said to Vivienne and the captain after the boys had gone to bed and they were sitting around the fireplace, enjoying the heat it was providing. "We built an excellent snowman, the captain is pleased with the horse he bought and last night two of the mares dropped beautiful, healthy bay colts. I've already had two people tell me if they were colts they would buy them. We're well on our way to improving the stock of horses in the area."

"And we're finally making some money on them," Vivienne added.

CHAPTER 12

"We got a letter from Mama today. She mentioned again how much it would mean to them if we could come for a visit this summer. Your parents came last summer but it's been almost two years since we've seen my parents. What do you think about the idea?" Vivienne asked Diego one night after they had gone to bed.

"That's a long trip, especially with the boys, for just a short visit."

"I know you can't get away for more than a few days but the boys have all summer. They get so bored with nothing to do for three months. If you wouldn't mind too much, I thought we could all go after school is out. You could stay for as long as you can and the boys and I could stay for several weeks."

"That's a long time to be apart."

"I know. We would all miss each other terribly but the boys have been asking me for months if they'll ever get to visit their grandparents."

"Have you said anything to them about going?"

"No. I wanted to see how you felt about the idea before I said anything to them."

It was a long while before Diego said anything. "I'm sure the boys are anxious to go and I have no doubt you would enjoy the visit as much as they would. You're right, I can't be away for more than a few days at a time. The only solution I see is for the three of you to take the stage after school is out.

It will take you about a week to get there. I can get there in about half that time if I go by horseback. I can join you after you've been there awhile, then come back after a few days."

"Are you sure that's all right with you?" Vivienne asked, running her finger tips slowly across his bare chest, hoping he wouldn't change his mind.

"I won't like ya'll being away so long, but since I know how much it would mean to the three of you, it would be rather selfish of me to say you can't go."

"Oh, thank you!" Vivienne said. She was unable to keep the excitement out of her voice. "I'll write Mama in the morning and let them know we're coming, but I'm not going to say anything to the boys until just before we leave. And, please, don't you say anything to them either. They won't be able to think or talk about anything else after they find out about the trip."

"I promise I won't say anything to them. Now let's stop talking. Come here and let me show you what you'll be missing while you're gone," Diego said. He pulled her close and his hands slowly and deliberately began roaming over her body. Their lips met and all thoughts of Black Creek were forgotten.

Vivienne was in the parlor mending one of Charlie Joe's shirts and thinking about their trip to Black Creek. It was only a month away. *I'm really going to enjoy being back in civilization, if only for a few weeks.* It got harder every day not to say anything to Travis and Charlie Joe about the trip. *Diego was right. I'm almost as excited about the trip as the boys were going to be.*

The boys were outside playing and making more noise than she thought possible for two little boys to make. Suddenly, it got very quiet. She was about to go see what was going on when Charlie Joe came into the room and plopped down heavily in the chair next to the door. The look on his face told her something was troubling him. Knowing her son as she did, she knew it wouldn't be long before he told her what was on his mind.

Sure enough, in a couple of minutes, without looking up, he quietly asked, "Why do you love Travis more than you do me?"

"I don't love him more than you. I love you and your brother just the same. Why do you ask such a thing?"

Still looking down at his feet he said, "Because you're always whipping me and yelling at me, and you never whip Travis."

Vivienne put her sewing down, and went over to her son. She put her arm around him, and gave him a hug. "Sweetheart, your papa and I love you and your brother the same. Travis gets his share of discipline. Think about this, if it sometimes seems you get disciplined more often than he does, maybe it's because you get into more mischief and talk back more often than he does."

"Am I badder than him?" he asked.

"No. You're just a little more curious and mischievous. We correct you because we want to be sure you understand what behavior is right and what is wrong. If we didn't love you, we wouldn't care what you did."

"Then you don't love Travis more than you do me?" he asked, looking at her for the first time.

"No," she answered, tousling his hair.

"Good." Suddenly a bright smile lit his face. With that he got up and ran outside, letting the back door slam loudly behind him. *At least he closed the door*, she thought with a smile.

Something made him ask that question and I think I know what it might have been. I'm going to have to sit Travis down and have a talk with him. She wondered exactly what Travis had said and how she was going to respond.

"This afternoon Charlie Joe asked me why I love Travis more than I do him," Vivienne told Diego that evening after the boys had gone to bed.

"What did you tell him?"

"I told him we love them both the same. Knowing there was a reason for his question, I talked to Travis about it later. He finally admitted he had been mad at Charlie Joe and had told him we love him more because he doesn't get as many whippings. I then had a long talk with Travis about how we love both of them the same and he should never tell Charlie Joe otherwise. Hopefully, both were satisfied with my answers."

"I was just a little older than Charlie Joe is now when Antonio and I thought our parents loved Miguel more than they did us. It never occurred to either of us at the time the reason Miguel seldom got in trouble with our parents was because, like Travis, he seldom did anything he shouldn't. I guess that's a question all brothers and sisters have at one time or another," Diego said with a smile.

"Only the mischievous ones. I'm sure Miguel never had that thought," Vivienne told him.

"Most likely not."

"Maybe I shouldn't fuss at Charlie Joe as often as I do," Vivienne said thoughtfully.

"Please don't do that," Diego laughed. "You never discipline him unless it's absolutely necessary. I don't want him to become spoiled and get by with more than he does already.

"I've always known parents can put guilt on their children," Diego said thoughtfully. "I'm just now finding out children can put guilt on their parents as well."

"Maybe I should show Charlie Joe more often that I love him," Vivienne said.

"Don't do anything different than you're doing now. You're an excellent mother and don't ever forget it," Diego said as he put a kiss on her cheek.

"Thank you, dear. You're also an excellent father."

"Thank you. Since we're both such excellent parents we should have perfect children!"

"I'm afraid we have a long way to go before we can claim that," she laughed.

"Today, when I was walking past the school, Mr. Barnes stopped me and asked if I would like to help in the schoolroom this fall. I told him I would need to talk to you about it before I could give him an answer," Vivienne told Diego the next day.

"What would you be doing?" he asked.

"Helping the younger children with their reading and arithmetic. And, helping Mr. Barnes grade the students' papers."

"Is it something you want to do?"

"Yes. I would enjoy it very much. Besides that, I would feel I was doing something worthwhile. Although the school is small, Mr. Barnes doesn't have the time he needs to help all the children. Many of them need extra attention because they are unable to attend school on a regular basis. And so many speak very little English. While I'm helping them with their English, it will help me with my Spanish.

"Learning Mr. Barnes' teaching techniques will enable me to help Travis and Charlie Joe more effectively when they need help with their school work.

"It will also give me something to do during the day while the boys are in school and you aren't here." *And it will keep me from spending so much time worrying about you, and the dangers in this barren, dangerous land where we're living*, she thought.

"It seems you've put a lot of thought into this. As long as it doesn't take away from the time you spend with the boys, I don't see any reason for you not to help Mr. Barnes."

"Thank you. I also promise it won't take from the time I spend with you," she assured him. She put her arms around his neck and gave him a playful kiss.

"I wonder how the boys will feel about you being at the school?"

"I doubt Travis will mind, or even notice, but I'm sure Charlie Joe won't like it a bit. Mr. Barnes will probably be grateful for another set of eyes watching him. He's such a little rounder, I know he's bound to be a challenge for Mr. Barnes."

"If he's not a challenge for Mr. Barnes, he's the only person Charlie Joe doesn't challenge," Diego laughed.

"What happened to you?" Vivienne asked a few days later when Diego came into the house and she noticed his torn and dirty shirt and pants.

"That damn horse threw me!" he grumbled under his breath.

"What caused him to do that?" she asked.

"A javelina came from behind a bush and startled him and he went crazy."

"I didn't think there was a horse alive that could throw you!" she said, trying, without success to suppress a smile. She wanted to ask which horse it was that had thrown him but she didn't want to add to his humiliation.

"At least he stayed around so you didn't have to walk home."

"If he hadn't ground tied, like he'd been trained to do, I would of shot him."

She didn't say anything but she knew he would never have done that.

"If you'll take your clothes off and clean up, I'll go get you some clean clothes. Apparently, all that's hurt is your pride," she said. She lit a fire in the kitchen stove and put a kettle of water on the burner to heat for his bath.

"Wipe that silly grin off your face," he grumbled. He cast her a dark look that only made the situation more humorous to her.

"Yes, dear," she said as she turned to leave the room. When she reached the bedroom she shut the door and burst into laughter. *Hurt pride can be rather painful at times*, she thought, *but it can also be rather funny.*

When she had herself under control she went back into

the kitchen and found Diego in the washroom pouring water in the tub for his bath.

"Are you sure you're not hurt?" she asked.

"I'm fine," he grumbled.

"Do you want me to put some alcohol on those scrapes on your arms?" she asked.

"No!"

With that he handed her the empty kettle and got into the tub.

Chapter 13

"Mmm, that was good!" Diego said after several long kisses. "I've missed you."

"I've missed you too. More than you will ever know," Vivienne said. "You've never been gone that long before. Did you and Captain Jones catch the bank robbers?"

"Don't we always get our man?" he asked in a serious tone. Then a grin crossed his face.

"We also found out why the bank had been robbed twice in the past month and why the stagecoach had been held up several times lately when it was carrying a large sum of money. It seems one of the bank tellers, who knew when the stagecoach would be carrying a large payroll, as well as when the bank's safe would be full, was passing that information to the robbers. He was receiving a cut of the take for his information.

"After we figured that out, and arrested the teller, he became a fountain of information. He told us who the robbers were and where their hideout was. I guess he figured if he was going to spend time in prison, they should too."

"You and the captain make a good team."

"Yes, it seems we do. I really enjoyed the investigating and interrogating we did."

"I know you also like tracking and finding the outlaws. Is there any part of being a Ranger you don't like?"

"I like everything about being a Ranger except the time I'm away from you and the boys."

"Thank you for the letters you wrote. They kept me from worrying so much while you were away. The boys liked them too. It was thoughtful of you to include each of them in every letter. They really enjoyed the adventures you shared. Knowing your imagination, I couldn't help wondering how true some of those stories were."

"I swear, everything I said was the gospel truth," he said. She knew he was feigning the innocent look.

"However, I will admit, some of the stories might have been exaggerated just a little."

"I though so," she said with a smile.

"How did everything go while I was gone? Did the boys behave themselves?"

"They behaved as well as could be expected. Except for Charlie Joe nearly getting bit by a rat when he went to get some feed out of the barrel for the chickens, everything else went very smoothly."

"Those things happen. I'll bet it gave him a good scare!" Diego laughed.

"You wouldn't think it was so funny if he had been bitten."

"The point is he wasn't, and it taught him to look in the barrel before sticking his hand in there. Anywhere there's feed, you'll find varmints. Just be glad it wasn't a snake. I guess we either need to get another barn cat or a more secure lid on the feed barrel, or both," Diego admitted, when he saw the look on her face.

What's it going to take before he realizes how dangerous it is for the boys living out here? Vivienne wondered.

Deciding it was best to change the subject she said, "We got an interesting letter from Captain Jones' wife the other day. She said they would like to come for a visit next month, if it's all right with us. Of course, I told her we would love to have them. I've been wanting to meet her and Louise for some time.

"While you were with Captain Jones did he say anything to you about them coming?"

"No. I guess he was leaving it up to you ladies to make all the plans. However, he did mention that Louise is finishing her schooling this year. I guess the trip here is sort of a gift to her to celebrate the occasion. When are they coming?"

"I told her anytime would be fine with us, but suggested the first part of June."

"Is their visit going to interfere with your plans to go to Black Creek?"

"No. I haven't told the family exactly when to expect us. Mrs. Jones said they would only be here for a few days. We can go after they leave and still have plenty of time with the family."

"Have you told the boys they're coming?"

"Yes. They're excited about the captain coming. They really do like him. But they're not too excited about having two more women in the house." They both got a hearty laugh from that remark.

The day the coach was due from San Angelo, Diego stayed home. When they heard the stage come into town, he quickly hitched up the buggy. He and the boys then went to the station to greet the Jones family and bring them to the house for their visit.

"Mrs. Jones, Louise, I'd like you to meet my wife, Vivienne," Diego said as he entered the house with the Joneses.

"It's so nice of you to have us. T. P. has told us so many nice things about you and the boys, I just had to meet you. I want to thank you for making T. P. feel so comfortable when he's here."

"It's our pleasure. We all enjoy his visits. When he's here, our home is his home and, of course, he is Travis and Charlie Joe's hero," Vivienne told her.

"I hope you don't think it was rude of me for inviting ourselves."

"Not at all, I've been wanting to meet you and Louise. I'm sorry I didn't invite you earlier but I didn't think you would want to make that long trip just to visit with us.

"I hope the boys didn't bother you. I'm sure they talked non-stop from the time they arrived at the station until you got here," Vivienne said.

"They weren't a bother at all. We thoroughly enjoyed them. They're both quite delightful."

"You may change your mind about that before your visit is over," Vivienne chuckled.

"Papa said when I was their age I talked more and asked more questions than they do," Louise told her.

"That's hard to believe," Vivienne laughed.

"Louise," Travis said shyly, as he looked at her in awe, "you're beautiful." "Oh! Thank you," she said quietly as a blush crossed her face and she glanced at her mother.

"Travis, I agree with you completely," Captain Jones said, smiling.

"Louise, you'll find not only are both of these young men rather outspoken, neither of them say anything they don't mean," the captain told his daughter.

"Captain, you're embarrassing Louise," Vivienne said, as she saw Louise's face turn an even deeper shade of red.

"I didn't know a woman could be embarrassed by too many compliments," he said.

"In spite of what you and Diego may think, we can.

"Now, let's get you all settled in your rooms. When you've had time to rest for a bit, we can have supper. After all those days traveling, I'm sure you're ready for some home cooked food."

"That sounds wonderful! We did have some meals along the way that weren't very good, to say the least. I hope our being here isn't going to crowd you," Mrs. Jones said.

"Not at all. We have four bedrooms. The boys are going to double up but they don't mind doing that. Do you?" she asked. She looked at them with a look they had seen often enough to know not to protest about the sleeping arrangements.

"Mrs. Jones, Louise, if either of the boys bother you or say anything you don't like, please feel free to correct them," Vivienne told them, as they were going into the dining room a little later.

"Please, don't worry about that. I'm sure they won't," Mrs. Jones assured her.

"Louise, now that you have finished your schooling do you have any plans for your future?" Vivienne asked.

"Kind of," she said looking at her father. "There's a young man who has been courting me and I think he's going to ask for my hand in marriage. My parents like him very much and approve of him."

"Is he your age?" Vivienne asked.

"No ma'am. He's twenty-two. He's an accountant in Christoval. But, he's talking about moving to San Angelo."

"How did the two of you meet?" Vivienne asked.

"He's the older brother of a friend of mine. We have all known him and his family for a long time."

"If you should marry him, I know your parents will be glad to have you living in San Angelo. I hope you have many happy years together."

"Thank you ma'am."

"I'm glad we're going to have some time to talk without our husbands being around," Vivienne said to Elizabeth the next afternoon. The men had taken the boys and gone out to the Hidalgo's so the captain could see the mares and their foals.

"I hope you don't mind Louise going to her room and reading. The trip seems to have tired her more than it did me. And she does love to read."

"Not at all. I want all of you to make our home yours while you're here."

"You look like there's something in particular you want to talk about," Elizabeth said, looking at Vivienne. "Does it have anything to do with being married to a Texas Ranger?"

"Yes," Vivienne said quietly.

"If you're wondering, whether you'll ever stop worrying about Diego when he's away on an assignment or won't miss him, the answer is no. After a while you'll learn to accept those things, but you'll never stop worrying or missing him. I'm sure, even when he's home, you find yourself worrying about his next assignment."

"Yes, I do. Between that and the dangers this untamed territory presents the boys, I sometimes feel it's more than I can bear."

"T. P. and I were both rather surprised when we learned a Ranger with a young family had accepted an assignment to this area. In the past, they always sent an unmarried man to this part of the state."

"Diego had wanted to become a Texas Ranger since he was a small boy. Being his first assignment, I think he was afraid if he didn't accept it the Rangers wouldn't give him another chance. And, of course, he enjoys the challenges and dangers the territory presents him."

"The men don't seem to understand how hard their occupation is on their wives. I've often wondered how T. P. can bear the hardships he goes through when he's out on an assignment. He complains about the bad food, the weather, and sleeping on the ground. But I've noticed after he's been home for just a short while, he gets restless and is ready to go again. I'm sure you've noticed the same thing with Diego."

"Yes, I have. The boys miss him terribly when he's gone. They don't understand and it's hard for me to explain to them that he misses them also."

"The affect their absences have on their children is another thing that's hard on us. I'm sure it's harder on your boys, having their father away so much of the time, than it was on Louise."

"Thank you for understanding. I'm glad to know I'm not the only one who feels this way."

"Oh, believe me, you aren't alone!" Elizabeth assured her.

"At least San Angelo is a large enough town where there are things to keep me busy while T. P. is away. Apache Flats is so small there's nothing for you to do while Diego is away, except worry."

"Yes, and that's exactly what I do. This coming school year I'm going to help the school teacher with the younger students several mornings a week. That will give me something to do and hopefully keep me from worrying so much. Well, enough about my problems," Vivienne said. "I need to go to the General Store to get some supplies for dinner tonight. Would you like to go with me and meet our friends, Teresa and Joaquin Navarro? They own and operate the store. Teresa is anxious to meet you. Maybe Louise will be up to going with us."

"Yes, I would enjoy going with you. I'm sure Louise will also enjoy the opportunity."

When they got to the General Store Vivienne introduced Elizabeth and Louise to Teresa. Teresa said, "It's a real pleasure to meet you Mrs. Jones. Mr. Jones has been in here several times and we thoroughly enjoy him. He is such a gentleman."

"Thank you. Vivienne has also told us many nice things about you and your family."

"I can't tell you how pleased we are with the job Diego is doing. We all feel much safer since he has been assigned to the area."

The three women had just returned from the General Store when T. P., Diego and the boys came riding up. A mare and a pretty little gray filly were tied to the back of the wagon.

"Louise, you've been wanting a younger and more spirited horse. I think I've found you one. It'll be a couple of years before she's old enough for you to ride but I think she's just what you've been wanting," T. P. told his daughter.

"Oh, thank you, Papa! She's a beautiful little lady," Louise said. She went over to the filly and began petting her. "That's what I'm going to name her, Lady Gray."

"Diego is going to start her training now, and next spring, when she's a yearling, he'll take her to Sonora. I'll meet him there and take her to San Angelo."

"Thank you Mr. Black. I know you can train her better than anyone in San Angelo," Louise told him.

Chapter 14

"Vivienne, has Diego said anything to you about taking your boys to Flat Rock?" the captain asked that evening when she came back into the room, after telling the boys good night.

"He mentioned it. But I told him in no uncertain terms he was not going to do that!"

"You know how much the boys would enjoy seeing a ghost town. Captain Jones said he would go with us. How much better protection can they have than two Texas Rangers?" Diego pointed out.

"You ladies are welcome to come along. After we look through Flat Rock, there's a small town close by where we can stay the night, so we won't need to come home after dark," Captain Jones added.

"T. P., this is something between Diego and Vivienne. I think it best if you keep your thoughts to yourself," Elizabeth gently chided him.

Seeing the pleading expression on Diego's face, Vivienne couldn't help but smile. He had never begged for anything but, there was no doubt in her mind he was ready to do just that if she didn't change her mind and agree to let him take the boys to the ghost town.

"You really want to take the boys, don't you?" she asked.

"Yes, I do."

"Elizabeth, if I change my mind about them going, would you and Louise be willing to go with us? I'm not about to let them go without me. Even if they are under the protection of two Texas Rangers."

"Don't let these two fast talking men convince you to do something you don't feel right about," Elizabeth said, looking at T. P.

"I'm not. The look on Diego's face is like looking at Travis and Charlie Joe. He'll enjoy taking them as much as they'll enjoy going. I also know how much the boys would love to see a ghost town."

"If you're sure, then yes, we'll go with you. T. P. has wanted Louise and me to go there for quite awhile."

"Thank you."

"Shall we go in the morning?" Diego asked eagerly. He didn't want to give Vivienne a chance to change her mind. When everyone agreed he smiled and said, "Don't anyone mention anything about hearing the ghost's music. I want to see if either of the boys hear it, without knowing about it."

"You haven't said anything to them about that?" Captain Jones asked in surprise.

"No. I didn't want to mention it to them until they had a chance hear it for themselves."

"In other words you knew I would eventually give in to your request to let them go," she said.

"I was hoping," he admitted with a guilty smile

The next morning Vivienne got the boys up before dawn. "Why did we have to get up so early when school's out? I'm still sleepy," Charlie Joe complained. He rubbed the sleep from his eyes, as he and Travis came into the kitchen for breakfast.

"We thought you might like to go to Flat Rock to see a ghost town," Diego told the boys.

Suddenly, both boys were fully awake. They were so excited they could hardly sit still long enough to eat breakfast.

During the trip to Flat Rock when the boys weren't talking about what they would see in the ghost town they were asking how much longer it would be until they got there.

"Louise, if you want to get out and see the ghost town with us, I'll protect you. You can hold my hand if you get scared," Travis told her.

"That's so brave of you, Travis, but I believe I'll stay in the buggy with Mama and your mother," Louise told him.

Sweet Louise, Vivienne thought. *She's being so kind to Travis and taking his adoration of her so gracefully. I'll have to let her know how much I appreciate her graciousness.*

When they pulled up in front of what had been the general store in Flat Rock both boys jumped out of the buggy.

"I want both of you to stay close to Captain Jones or myself all the time," Diego said. He took both of the boys' hands and knelt down in front of them. Looking them in the eyes he said, "If either of you run ahead, you'll finish the afternoon in the buggy with the ladies! Have I made myself clear?"

"Yes, sir." Travis said.

"Remember, a man always stands by his word," Diego told them.

"Charlie Joe?" Diego asked after a long moment of silence.

"I promise," he said solemnly.

"Okay. Now, let's check out this ghost town!" Diego said smiling, as he stood up.

They had looked in every building they passed and were about half-way down one side of the street when Charlie Joe suddenly froze in his tracks. "I hear a piano playing," he said quietly.

"You're *loco*. This is a ghost town. There's no one here to play a piano," Travis told him.

Diego looked at the captain and smiled before saying anything. "If he's *loco*, the captain and I are too. We've also heard the music." He then proceeded to tell the boys about the legend of the piano player.

"Why didn't I hear it?" Travis asked, in disappointment.

"No one knows the answer to that question," the captain told him. "Sometimes a person hears the music and sometimes he doesn't. I didn't hear it the first time I was here or the time your father and I came, but I have heard it several times."

"I don't hear it now either but I did hear it the first time I was here," Diego told him.

"Can I go tell Mama I heard it?" Charlie Joe asked.

"Yes. We'll finish looking in the rest of the buildings when you get back," Diego told him.

At that Charlie Joe turned and ran to the buggy yelling, "I heard it! I heard the piano playing and nobody else did!"

When he reached the buggy, all out of breath and wide eyed, he told the ladies about hearing the ghost playing the piano.

"That's wonderful. I'm glad you got to hear it. Maybe your brother will hear it before we leave," his mother said.

"We're going to look in the other buildings now. Maybe, I'll see a ghost!" With that, he turned and ran back to where his brother and the men were waiting.

"The look on Charlie Joe's face just now was worth the trip out here," Elizabeth said, smiling at Vivienne.

"Yes, it was. I'm so glad one of the boys got to hear the music. I wish Travis could have heard it as well. I know he's disappointed."

"You know, not hearing the music today will make Travis want to come back," Elizabeth told her.

"I know," Vivienne said, and let out a sigh.

"T. P.'s been trying to get Louise and me to come here since the first time he heard the music. I know he's disappointed we chose to stay in the buggy."

"If the two of you would like to go with them, I don't mind staying here by myself," Vivienne told her.

"Thank you, but I have no desire to either see or hear a ghost," Elizabeth told her.

"I wonder if we would hear the music if we went down the street?" Louise asked.

"Do you want to go?" Elizabeth asked her.

"No!" All I'd probably hear would be a rattlesnake," she said with a shiver.

"Louise I want to thank you for handling Travis' admiration of you in such a sweet, ladylike way."

"Oh, it's no trouble. He's such a sweet boy. I certainly don't want to hurt his feelings," she said.

In spite of not hearing the music again or seeing a ghost, all the boys could talk about on the ride to the boarding house, where they would be staying the night, was the ghost town.

"Elizabeth, I want to thank you and Louise for coming with us. If you hadn't agreed to come, I don't think I would have consented to let Diego and the captain bring the boys."

"Oh, it was fun," Louise told her. "Now I can tell all my friends I've been to a ghost town."

"Are you going to tell them you stayed in the buggy the whole time you were there?" her father asked, with a wink and a smile.

"Not unless they ask," she said, returning his smile.

"Boys, I think you should thank the ladies as well," Diego told his sons.

"Thank you!" they both said. They gave Elizabeth and Louise their biggest smiles.

Yes. It was well worth the trip, Vivienne thought as she looked at the two happy little boys.

The Joneses stayed a few more days before going back to San Angelo. The two families parted as good friends.

A few evenings after the Joneses left, Vivienne told Diego she was going to tell the boys the next day about the trip to

Black Creek.

"Are you sure you want to tell them so soon? It's still over a week before you leave," Diego said.

"I know, but I've got to start packing and getting things ready for the trip and they'll want to know what I'm doing. I don't want to lie to them.

"While we're gone try not to take advantage of Teresa and Joaquin's hospitality."

"That shouldn't be a problem. I don't plan on being home anymore than I have to while you're gone."

Chapter 15

"The boys aren't even here yet and you've already started spoiling them," Maria said, as Seth and Jace rode up to the house leading two ponies.

"Grandmothers aren't the only ones who can spoil grandchildren," Jace informed her.

"The boys are going to be thrilled to have the ponies to ride while they're here. You know, of course, when they go back to Apache Flats, they're going to want to take the ponies with them but they won't be able to."

"Why not?" Seth asked.

"Because, they're still too young to be riding by themselves. Especially around Apache Flats. Since Diego is away from home so much of the time, who would ride with them?"

"Oh, I guess we didn't think about that," Seth said, as a guilty look crossed his face.

Jace didn't say anything but Maria noticed he was giving her one of his dark looks. She had realized before that he didn't like being told he had done something wrong, especially by a woman. She tried to be very diplomatic when she was talking with him, but it wasn't always easy.

"It looks like I'll be taking the ponies to Miguel's to stay until we're ready to give them to the boys," Seth said.

"Don't tell the boys the ponies are theirs. Just tell them they can ride them while they are here. And, please, do Vivienne a favor and don't let the boys know about the ponies until the day after they arrive. I don't think she could stand their excitement until she's had a day to rest," Maria advised them.

"Amber said to tell you we'll pick the family up in San Antonio Friday afternoon and take them to our house for the night. We'll bring them out here Saturday morning," Jace told her.

"That sounds good. Thank you," Maria replied. "I hope you and Amber plan to stay out here for the rest of the day."

"I'll tell Amber. I'll take the ponies to Miguel's on the way home," Jace replied.

"I would like for Vivienne and the boys to stay here in the house with us but she may feel more comfortable staying in the little house where they lived before moving to Apache Flats. I'm going to leave the choice up to her," Maria said to Seth after Jace left.

"When I told the other grandchildren Travis and Charlie Joe were coming for a visit, Matthew and Daniel were thrilled. Selena, on the other hand, wasn't happy about two more boys to contend with. The poor little girl will be out-numbered four to one," Maria added.

"Don't worry about Selena," Seth laughed. "That young lady will be able to handle those four boys quite well."

"I can't believe we're finally here." Vivienne said, as she got out of the stage coach in San Antonio and gave her mother a hug.

"Oh, Papa, it's so good to see you. I've missed the two of you so much."

"We've missed you too," Jace said.

"Travis, Charlie Joe, you've both grown so much, since I last saw you," Amber said as she gave each of them a hug.

"I'm taller than Travis," Charlie Joe said proudly.

"My goodness, so you are."

"It's a good thing we brought the Black's coach. We never would have been able to get all this stuff in our buggy," Jace said, as he and a cowboy put the trunk and bags Vivienne had brought on top of the coach.

"Are you going to sit inside the coach with us?" Travis asked his grandfather.

"Do you want me to?" he asked.

"Yes!" both boys answered.

"Then I guess I will. We'd better get rolling, if we want to get home before dark," he said. He then opened the door of the coach and helped Amber and Vivienne step inside.

"I didn't expect to see you until we got to the ranch," Vivienne told her mother when they had settled in the coach.

"I wasn't about to wait another two hours to see the three of you. I wish Diego could have come with you. When is he going to be able to get here?" Amber asked.

"He should be here in a couple of weeks."

Before she could say any more, both of the boys started telling their grandparents all about what they had been do-ing since they had been living in Apache Flats.

When they finally stopped talking Jace noticed Travis seemed to be studying him. Finally, Travis said, "There was an Indian at the church the other day who looked just like you."

"You haven't told them?" Jace asked, looking at Vivienne.

"No."

"Well then, I guess it's up to me to do that. The reason for that is because I'm half Indian. My mother was an Apache. Before you ask," Jace said giving them one of his rare smiles, "no, I've never scalped anyone."

"Did you ever live with the Indians?" Travis asked.

"After my mother died I spent a year living with her fam-ily. I decided then I liked living in the white mans' world better."

"Do you know how to talk Apache?" Charlie Joe asked.

"Yes."

"Will you teach us?" Travis asked.

"If you really want to learn the language I guess I can do that."

"Yes!" Travis said excitedly.

As they approached Jace and Amber's house on the ranch Vivienne noticed that the boys' conversations had slowed down and they were both yawning. After eating, they both immediately went to bed without being told.

"It doesn't happen often," Vivienne told her parents after she had gone to tell the boys good night, "but, by the time I told them good night, they were both asleep. Now we can have a nice quiet conversation."

"The boys have grown so much since you moved to Apache Flats. But that's the only thing that's changed. Travis still has trouble getting a word in edgewise when Charlie Joe's around," Amber said.

"I've been trying to teach them not to interrupt someone when they're talking but sometimes interrupting Charlie Joe is the only way Travis has a chance to say anything."

"We're going to take you to Maria and Seth's in the morning so you can stay out there. I wish you could stay here with us, but you'll have more room there and be more comfortable."

"We got both the boys a pony to ride while they're here," Jace told her.

"Oh Papa, thank you. They'll be thrilled. They don't get a chance to ride very often at home. We don't have horses for them yet, but I know it won't be long before we'll need to do that."

"When the boys are old enough to be riding alone let us know and we'll send the ponies to them," Amber said.

"Thank you for the offer but it would be so expensive having them transported all the way to Apache Flats, I'm sure when the time comes we'll be able to find horses that are suitable for them closer to home."

"We have some more good news for you. We found out a few days ago Miranda is going to have a baby."

"Oh, that's wonderful. I know she and Antonio are both

excited. They've waited so long."

The next morning Vivienne awoke to the sound of the boys telling their grandparents more about their adventures in Apache Flats. *I wish I could get rested up as quickly as they do*, she thought. Reluctantly, she got out of bed and started dressing.

When she went into the kitchen, the boys each told her a quick good morning, then continued their stories. Except for the trip to Flat Rock, most of what they were telling were things she had been trying to forget.

After breakfast, while Vivienne and Amber were washing the dishes, Vivienne told her mother about some of the dangers they faced daily in Apache Flats.

"Besides the dangers, I'm concerned about the education the boys are getting. There is only one teacher for the thirty some odd students. He doesn't have the time to give each grade the attention it needs. This fall I'm going to help teach the younger grades, and help the other students as much as I can. Hopefully, that will give Mr. Barnes more time to spend with the higher grades."

After they finished cleaning the kitchen, they went out on the porch to finish their conversation and watch the boys play.

"Are you ready to go to Seth and Maria's?" Jace asked a little later when he went up on the porch.

"I think so. You and Mama are going to stay out there for a while aren't you?"

"Yes. If the boys will come help me, I'll hitch up the coach and we can be on our way." With that, Jace and two happy little boys went to the barn.

The coach had not come to a complete stop in front of the house on Black Creek when Travis and Charlie Joe jumped out and ran into the house. Jace had just helped Vivienne and Amber down and was getting the luggage out of the coach when Maria and Seth came out of the house. After greeting them and giving each a hug, Vivienne asked where Travis and Charlie Joe had gone.

"After a quick hello to us they asked where Matthew was. When I told them he was probably in his house, they ran out the back door looking for him. Grandparents come in second to cousins they haven't seen in two years," Maria laughed.

"I'm sorry," Vivienne apologized. "We have tried to teach them manners, but they don't always remember."

"Don't give it a second thought," Maria said. "They wouldn't be little boys if they had acted any other way."

"Does Matthew know about the surprise we have for Travis and Charlie Joe?" Jace asked.

"Are you kidding? Matthew can't keep a secret any better than any other six-year- old boy. We didn't even tell Selena. Of course, Daniel knows since they're keeping the ponies in their barn."

"We thought, as soon as you have a chance to unpack and catch your breath, we'd all go to *El Rio Negro* and you could visit with Miguel and Lila while Antonio and Jace take Travis and Charlie Joe for a ride. Or, if you would rather, we can wait until tomorrow," Maria told her.

"Now is fine. The longer we wait, the more likely someone will accidentally say something and spoil the surprise about the ponies."

"You can stay here with Miranda if you'd rather," Maria said.

"I'll go with you. I want to see their faces when they get the ponies. Aren't you going with us?" she asked Miranda.

"No thank you. I'm not getting in anything that moves until after this baby is born," Miranda said putting her hand on her stomach. "I can't even stand the motion of a rocking chair."

"Hopefully, you'll get over that in another month. I know I did," Vivienne told her.

"Do you mind if I go?" Antonio asked Miranda.

"Of course not. I'll go take a nap while ya'll are gone."

"Is Miranda having trouble with her pregnancy?" Vivienne quietly asked Maria once when they were outside.

"No. The doctor says everything is fine. It's just that this is her first baby and she is almost thirty. Doctor Brown thinks that's the reason she's having such a problem with being queasy."

"I hope everything goes all right for her."

"I'm sure it will," Maria assured her.

"Selena is almost as excited about the baby as Miranda and Antonio are. However, she has said if it's a boy she's going to run away from home. She seems to think a brother and four boy cousins is more than she can handle."

"I can certainly understand that. Aren't Victoria and Selena going with us?" Vivienne asked as they got into the buggy.

"No. There's not enough room in the buggies for anymore. Victoria wants to stay here with Miranda, and Selena has no desire to spend the afternoon with four little boys. The reason Matthew is going is because he wants to play with his cousins. He didn't say anything, but I imagine he also wants to show them what a good rider he is."

When they reached *El Rio Negro* and Seth and Jace helped Maria and Vivienne out of the buggy. Seth whispered, "Would you see to it the boys stay inside while we get their ponies saddled and bring them to the house?"

With that the women and boys went inside and greeted Lila and Miguel. A few minutes later, Seth came inside and said, "Would you boys come outside for a minute? I need your help with something."

When everyone went out, Antonio and Jace were standing in front of the house holding the reins of Daniel's pony and two sorrel ponies.

"Well, do you like them?" Jace asked. Charlie Joe and Travis stood on the porch, speechless, looking in awe at the ponies.

"Are they ours?" Travis finally asked.

"They're yours to ride while you're visiting here," Jace answered. He looked at Maria, obviously remembering what she had said about them not being able to take the horses back to Apaches Flats with them.

Suddenly, the boys ran down the porch steps. Each boy went to a different pony.

"Can we ride them now?" Charlie Joe asked.

"Yes. What are you going to name them," Seth asked.

"Mine's going to be named Flame," Charlie Joe told them proudly.

Travis looked at his pony carefully and said, "I'm going to name him Blaze."

"What appropriate names for two red ponies," Maria said.

"I wish Diego was here to share this moment with the boys," Vivienne said. She felt tears welling in her eyes over her sons' happiness.

"Do you think you two men can handle those four little guys?" Seth teasingly asked Antonio and Miguel.

"I think we can manage," Antonio answered. "Aren't you coming with us?"

"No thank you. My days of handling wild little boys is in the past. It's your turn."

"What about you, Jace?" Antonio asked.

"I'm staying here with him," Jace said, nodding his head toward Seth.

When the boys came in for lunch, all they could talk about was their ponies. Vivienne wasn't the least surprised when they got into an argument about which of them was the best rider. It seemed they argued about everything these days.

CHAPTER 16

As Diego rode the far western portion of his territory, he thought about Vivienne and the boys. He hadn't been home in a week; there was nothing to go home to. He missed his family even more at the house than he did here on the open range. This was a good time to patrol the areas he seldom got to because they were so far from Apache Flats and the family.

Suddenly, he heard gun shots. He turned his horse in the direction the shots were coming from. He soon saw a stagecoach racing down the road. It was being pursued by three men who were shooting at it.

Either there wasn't a shotgun rider or he had already been killed because no one was firing back from the stagecoach. All he saw was the driver, leaning down low and whipping the horses to run as fast as they could. Even at that, the three horsemen were gaining fast on the coach. Diego rode up behind the men chasing the coach, pulled out his pistol and starting shooting. Almost immediately, one of the men fell from his saddle. The other two men turned and started firing at Diego. As he fired the last bullet from his pistol, a second man fell to the ground. The third man turned his horse away from the coach and gave up his pursuit.

Diego pulled his rifle from the holster and took careful aim at the fleeing bandit. It took two shots, but the man suddenly slumped forward in the saddle, and dropped his horse's reins.

After a short chase, he caught the horse. The man wasn't dead, but he was wounded. Diego checked to see if the man was carrying another gun, besides the one he had dropped when he was shot, he didn't find one. He took the horse's reins and turned back to the road. He stopped to pick up one of the other men he had shot and found the man was dead. After catching the man's horse, he put him across the saddle and headed back to where the coach was waiting.

"Thanks, Ranger," the driver said when Diego rode up to the coach and he saw the badge pinned to his shirt.

"Where's your shotgun rider?" Diego asked.

"Right here," he said. He pointed to the body of a man lying on the seat next to him.

"Dead?" Diego asked.

"'Fraid so."

"Have you got any passengers?"

"Nope. Jest a large payroll fer the Railroad. Looks like word got out about that."

"Looks like it. Let's put these two and the shotgun rider inside the coach. This one's not dead," he said as he helped the man from the saddle, "but I don't think he'll be giving you any trouble.

"After I go back and get the other man I shot, I'll come back and ride shotgun for you to Presidio. Word may have gotten to others you're carrying a big payroll."

"Thanks. There ain't nothing between here and Presidio 'cept lots 'a dust and men looking' fer trouble," the driver said, as he spit a wad of tobacco onto the ground.

After Diego returned he put the other outlaw inside the coach. "I'm Diego Black."

"People call me, Pete," the driver said.

"You from around these parts?" Diego asked.

"Hell, no. Ain't nobody with a lick of sense lives out here. Guess you might say I'm from Angelo."

"San Angelo. Do you know Captain T. P. Jones?"

"Know of him. Ain't never come face to face with him.

Heard he's a mighty fine man."

"That he is." Diego tied his horse and those of the outlaws to the back of the stagecoach then climbed on top of the coach next to the driver. He settled in for the long, hot dusty ride into Presidio.

Seth and Antonio had taken the boys for a ride and Vivienne was visiting with Victoria and Selena. Suddenly, they heard Charlie Joe shouting, "Papa's here, Papa here."

Vivienne ran out the door and saw the boys and three men riding up to the house. One of those men was Diego. She shouted his name and ran toward him. He jumped from his horse, grabbed her and whirled her around.

"I didn't expect to see you so soon," she said.

"I couldn't wait another day to see you," he said. Then gave her a passionate kiss.

"How long are you going to be able to stay," she asked.

"Two weeks," he said as he put her down. "Sergeant Kelton is going to handle my territory while I'm gone and Captain Jones is watching over Sergeant Kelton's and his own territory."

"Dear, Captain Jones. What would we do without him? The boys and I are going back with you. We've all been miserable without you," she told him.

"The boys told me the ponies were theirs to ride while they're here but they can't take them to Apache Flats. Do you think they're going to be willing to leave them so soon?"

"I'm not going to give them a choice," she said and laughed.

"We weren't expecting you for at least another week," Maria said as she and Seth came out of the house. She gave Diego a hug. "You look exhausted."

"I've been riding non-stop since I left home," he told her.

"So, you're not only tired and sleepy you're also starved," Vivienne said.

"You got that right. I'll eat anything you have. I don't even care if it's cooked."

"We were about to eat supper if you think you can wait about fifteen minutes," his mother told him.

"I'll be there as soon as I take care of my horses."

"Forget about the horses. I'll take care of them. I know I taught you to take care of your horse before taking care of your own needs, but this is one time I'll let you forget that rule. I'm not sure I want to sit at the dining table with you before you clean up a bit," Seth said smiling at his son.

"Thank you. This is one time I'll let you do that. Travis and Charlie Joe will help you, after they take care of their own horses," Diego said, looking at his sons.

"There's something wrong with Rafael," Diego said a few days after they had returned home from Black Creek.

"What makes you say that?" Vivienne asked.

"Well, I've noticed his grammar has been improving the past couple of months and he's asked me the meaning of several words lately. But, the real indication came just a few minutes ago. I ran into Lapopa and she asked why Rafael hasn't been to see her lately. I didn't know what to tell her."

"It's quite simple," she smiled. "He's in love."

"Rafael, in love? I find that hard to believe. Who's the lucky lady?"

"Esperanza Corrales."

"Are you sure? I would never have expected him to be interested in her."

"Why? Because she not seventeen years old and beautiful? Those are the very reasons I say he's in love. For the frst time he's looking at a woman more than skin deep. He's seeing all the reasons she would be a good wife."

"Is she interested in him?"

"Of course. What unmarried woman can resist him? Just because he's looking at her through the eyes of love doesn't mean he's not his usual charming self with her."

"He's known her for years. How come he's just now

noticing her?"

"Because, until now, he hasn't been ready to settle down and get married."

"Well I'll believe it when I see them walking down the aisle together."

"How was the first day back at school?" Vivienne asked Travis and Charlie Joe when they came into the house.

"It was good. There are a bunch of new kids in the school. One of them is in my class."

"And, Charlie Joe, how did your day go?"

"It was fine."

"What?" she asked in surprise. It was the first time she had ever asked him that question and gotten a positive answer.

"There's a new girl in his class and he's sweet on her," Travis said, then grinned.

"Am not!"

"Are too."

"Am not!"

"Charlie Joe's sweet on Katrina Fremont," Travis teased.

At that Charlie Joe doubled up his fist and took a swing at his brother. Fortunately for Travis, he saw Charlie Joe's fist coming and ducked before he was hit.

"All right you two that's enough," Vivienne said, as she stepped between the two boys. "If you don't behave yourselves I'm going to send both of you to your rooms."

"I'm going outside," Charlie Joe said. He gave his brother a glaring look, then turned and went out the door.

"I would advise you not to tease your brother about the girl," she told Travis.

"But he's so much fun to tease."

"You wouldn't have thought it was so much fun if I hadn't stopped him from hitting you and you had gotten a black eye."

"I don't know. It might have been worth it. He doesn't stand a chance with Katrina. All the boys in school are all mushy over her."

"Does that include you?"

"No."

"Oh. What does Katrina look like?"

"She has blond curly hair," Travis said.

"Is that all you can tell me about her?"

"I think she has blue eyes. I'm going outside," he said. He picked up a handful of cookies and turned toward the door.

"Give a couple of those cookies to your brother, and try not to tease him."

Before supper Vivienne told Diego about Charlie Joe's attraction for Katrina and asked him to please not tease him about her.

When they were all around the dinner table that evening Vivienne said, "I haven't told you two that I will be spending several mornings each week at the school."

"Why?" Charlie Joe asked.

Charlie Joe's response told them, without a doubt, he wasn't going to like his mother being at the school.

"I'll be helping the younger students with their reading and mathematics. You won't even know I'm there."

"When are you going to start?" Travis asked.

"Tomorrow. I'll go after you've already left for school. I promise I won't walk with you."

The next day after the boys had left and Vivienne had cleaned the kitchen she went to the school. The students were all settled in their chairs. While some were working on papers that Mr. Barnes had given them, others were listening to him give a history lesson.

After he finished the lesson he thanked Vivienne for coming and introduced her to the students. "Mrs. Black, today I would like for you to help the first and second graders with their mathematics. I've given them a sheet of paper with some problems which they have been working on. I'm sure by now some of them have questions for you."

She pulled her chair over to where the four students were sitting and asked if any of them needed help. They all said yes. She spent the morning working with those students on several subjects until it was time for lunch. She stayed a few minutes to let Mr. Barnes know how the morning had gone for her and to find out what he wanted her to do the next day. She went home happy, with a feeling of accomplishment.

"Well, how did school go for you today?" Diego asked Vivienne, when he came home that evening.

"Very good. I feel I really accomplished something. And I really enjoyed it."

"I'm glad to hear that," Diego said and grinned. "Just don't get to liking it so much you decide you want to teach every day. How did our sons behave?"

"To be perfectly honest I was so busy I didn't have time to even think about them. Oh. I told Mr. Barnes not to hesitate to discipline either of the boys while I'm there."

"I think they'll behave while you're there. At least for a day or two," Diego said.

"I'm glad you'll have something to occupy your time for a few days. I'm leaving tomorrow to patrol the far northern part of the territory. I'll be gone about a week."

One cold December day Diego came in the house smiling. "I just saw Charlie Joe and Katrina. They were walking down the street holding hands. Our youngest son does have good taste in women. She's a right pretty little lady."

"I can't believe it's been three months and he's still sweet on her. He's never stayed interested in anything that long,"

Vivienne said.

"What I can't believe is she's still interested in him. She's pretty enough to have any boy in the school."

"Why should that surprise you? He has his father's charm and good looks." She put her arms around him and kissed him.

"After being married to me for ten years do you still think I'm charming and good looking?" he asked grinning.

"Did I forget to mention you still have a lack of modesty?" she asked.

"By the way, we got a letter from your mother today and she had some good news. Miranda gave birth to a little girl."

"What did they name her?"

"Savannah Helena."

"I'm glad it was a girl. Now Selena won't have to run away from home," he teased.

CHAPTER 17

"Diego! Diego!" Vivienne screamed, running down the street toward him with Charlie Joe close behind her. "Some men just rode by and grabbed Travis and rode off with him!"

"How long ago?" he asked.

"About five minutes."

"Which direction?"

"That way!" she said, pointing east.

"You and Charlie Joe go to the General Store and stay with Joaquin and Teresa until I get back."

"You can't go by yourself. There were three of them!"

"I don't have time to form a posse," he said, impatiently. He turned his horse in the direction Vivienne had pointed.

"What's yer name, li'l feller?" one of the kidnappers demanded. He dragged Travis into a little shack, that was hidden in the middle of a strand of mesquite trees, a couple of miles out of town.

Travis didn't say anything. He just glared at the man.

"Tough li'l guy, ain't ya?" the man asked. "Well, we don't need to know yer name. We know yer the Ranger's boy an' whar' ya' live. We don't need to know no more.

"Yeow! The little brat bites!" the kidnapper yelled. He backhanded Travis and began tying his hands and feet together. He tore the bandana from around his own neck, and tied it around Travis' mouth so he couldn't yell.

He then sat down and began writing a note. "How ya' spell ransom?" he asked the other men.

"How the hell would we know?" one of them answered. "We ain't got no more schoolin' than ya' got."

He struggled for several minutes, trying to write the note. Finally, he folded it and handed it to one of the other men. "Here Jess, take this here note to tha' house where we got tha' kid. Then hightail it back here. We'll wait fer tha' Ranger to git our money to us. Then we'll kill 'em both." he smirked at Travis.

Jess took the note and set off on his mission.

"Your Ranger papa's gonna' make us rich," he laughed.

Travis just continued glaring at the man.

Diego followed the tracks of the three horses down the road for about a mile. Then the tracks left the road and he began following a trail that cut across the open land. *I'll be willing to bet they're headed for the little cabin that's tucked away in a small cluster of trees, not far from here*, he reasoned.

Suddenly, a lone rider came down the trail toward him. "Texas Ranger! Stop right where you are!" Diego called to the man.

Instead of stopping, Jess reached for his gun. But Diego's draw was faster. He shot before the rider's gun had cleared leather. His startled horse reared and the man tumbled to the ground.

Diego went to the fallen man and rolled him over. He saw his bullet had hit its mark. The man was dead. He searched the man's pockets and found the ransom note the other outlaw had written. It demanded five-hundred dollars for the safe return of Travis by the end of the day. *I wonder where they think, I'm going to get that kind of money in such a short time* he thought. He folded the note and put it in his shirt pocket.

"Just as I suspected, you were up to no good. Now I know for sure I'm on the right trail to my son. Your fresh tracks make the trail easier to follow."

He caught the loose horse and threw the man across the saddle then tied the horse to a tree. "I'll come back and get you after I get Travis," he said, as he patted the horse's shoulder.

A few minutes after Jess left the cabin the two remaining kidnappers heard the gunshot. "Go see what's hap'ning," Witt told the other man.

"I ain't going out there. I might git shot."

"If ya' don't go, I'm gonna' shoot ya' right here," Witt snarled.

Diego was watching the cabin from behind a group of small trees. He was wondering what his next move should be, when he saw one of the men slowly open the door and walk warily toward the horses tied in front of the cabin. Diego silently came up behind the man as he was mounting his horse. He raised his gun and hit the man over the head with the butt end of it.

Two down, one to go, Diego thought, as he watched the man crumble into an unconscious heap. *At least I hope there's only one more. The butt end of a gun works just as well as the barrel does without making near the noise. As hard as I hit him, he should be out for awhile,* Diego reasoned. He reached down and quickly removed the man's gun from its holster.

Then he quietly stole his way to the cabin's window. He rose slowly, and looked inside. He saw Travis lying on the floor of the cabin, bound and gagged. He seemed to be uninjured. On the other side of the room, the outlaw was sprawled out on the bunk bed. Looped over a chair, not far from where Travis lay, Diego saw the outlaw's gun belt with the gun still in the holster.

If the idiot had a lick of sense, he'd know not to take his gun belt off. My next move has to be fast and accurate, Diego thought.

He took a deep breath, and raised his gun and knocked out the window glass. He then shot at the man who had jumped off the bed when he heard the glass break. Gun still drawn, Diego was at the door and opened it before he even saw the man hit the floor.

"Travis," he said in relief. He grabbed his son and removed the gag from his mouth. "Are you all right?" he asked as he began untying him.

"That man hit me," Travis told him. He pointed to the man who lay on the floor with a bullet hole in the middle of his forehead. "But it didn't hurt."

"That's because you're tough," Diego told him.

A proud smile cross his son's face.

Vivienne's going to have a fit when she sees that red mark on your face, Diego thought when he saw the mark on Travis' face where the man had struck him.

As they were walking out the door, the man Diego had knocked out was just coming to.

Travis let go of Diego's hand and ran over to where the man was now sitting on the ground, rubbing his head, wondering what had happened. Travis lifted his leg back and kicked the man between his legs with all the force he had in him. The man let out a loud, painful yell. Before he could do anything but instinctively grab his crotch, Travis ran back to Diego with a big smile on his face.

"That wasn't very nice," Diego said, trying not to laugh.

"He's not a nice man," Travis stated in a matter-of-fact tone.

"I can't disagree with you about that. Now will you stay here and not move until I get that man tied up and the other man on his horse?"

"Yes sir. Where's the third man?" Travis asked.

"I took care of him before I got here."

"Oh! Did you shoot him?"

"Yes."

"Is he dead?"

"Yes."

"Good! He wasn't nice either."

"Papa," Travis said thoughtfully, as they were riding back to Apache Flats, "one of those mean men said they were going to get a lot of money from you and then they were going to kill both of us. But I wasn't scared. I knew you wouldn't let him do that."

That wasn't in the ransom note, but I was afraid that's what their intentions were, Diego thought to himself.

"Well, it looks like they're not going to be able to do that now, does it?"

"No. Is he going to jail?" Travis asked.

"Oh yes! For a long time." *If I have my way, he'll hang,* Diego thought.

"Good," Travis said.

"Son, I think it best if we not tell your mother the man said they were going to kill us. It would just worry her. We have to protect our women folk from worry as well as from danger."

"I won't tell her. I promise," Travis assured him.

"Papa. I think I know why that man hit me."

"And why was that?"

"Because I bit him. Was I bad to do that?"

"Under the circumstances, I don't think that was bad at all." *You little rascal,* Diego thought. *You bit one of the men and kicked another one where it hurt the most.* "Don't ever let anyone tell you, you're not full of spunk. You know, he might not have hit you if you hadn't bit him."

"That's okay. I hurt him more than he hurt me," Travis grinned.

"You probably did," Diego said with a chuckle.

It's strange, Diego thought. *I just killed two men and it didn't bother me in the least. I guess I've finally accepted that part of my job. Or, maybe it's because my son's life was in danger.*

When they rode up to the General Store, Vivienne came

running out the door. "Oh, my baby!" she cried as she grabbed Travis off the front of Diego's saddle and hugged him to her. "Are you all right?"

"I'm not a baby," he protested, trying to pull away.

"What happened to your face?" Vivienne asked in alarm when she saw the red mark on his cheek.

"That man over there hit me," he said, pointing to one of the men who was draped across his saddle. "But it didn't hurt."

The look Vivienne gave Diego at their son's remark told him she was going to have a lot to say about what Travis had just told her.

"I'll meet you back at the house when I get these three taken care of," Diego said. He turned the horses and headed for the jail, not looking forward to his upcoming confrontation with Vivienne.

"Where are the boys?" Diego asked when he came into the house, after taking the one kidnapper to the jail and the two dead men to the undertaker.

"They're in Travis' room playing. I may never let either of them outside the house again."

The expression on her face and her tone of voice told him she was still extremely upset over what had happened.

"I thought they were safe as long as I was with them but today proved that is not necessarily true. I wasn't ten feet from Travis when that man grabbed him and rode off with him.

"The dangers in this town are unbelievable. Besides killing a rattlesnake nearly every day, there are wolves coming into town, seemingly unafraid of people, killing pets and chickens, and even attacking horses. Then there are the shootouts in the saloons where a stray bullet might easily hit one of the boys, hurting them or even killing them, not to mention disgruntled Indians lurking around. I'm constantly on the lookout! I never know what's going to happen next! Not to mention a school where the boys are barely learning to read. I can't take anymore!"

"I'll admit all you said is true but, I think, you're exaggerating the circumstances a bit."

"I am not exaggerating and you know it! Don't try to downplay the dangers of living here. It's bad enough that you live in constant danger, but you are a grown man and have chosen to live that way. That's not the case with Travis and Charlie Joe. They don't have any choice except to live wherever we choose. They are just little boys, completely at our mercy.

"What if you hadn't ridden into town just minutes after Travis was grabbed? It might have been days before he was found, and more than likely, he would have been dead. Have you thought about that?" As she talked her voice grew louder and her tone became angrier and more frightened.

"There are other families with children living here and nothing has happened to any of them," Diego said in defense of the town.

"I don't care what has or has not happened to other families. All I care about is what just happened to our son. We were lucky this time. Next time it could be a lot worse. Whether you'll admit it or not, the fact you're a Ranger puts our children in more danger than the other children."

"What do you want me to do?" he asked.

"I want you to tell the Texas Rangers they can either send you somewhere more civilized or else you're going to resign."

"All right. I'll write Ranger Headquarters and see what they can do."

"You'll see what they can do?" she asked tersely as she glared at him. "That's mighty big of you! Did you actually listen to anything I just said? Don't you care what happens to your children?"

"You know damn well I care about them every bit as much as you do!"

"It certainly doesn't seem that way. It seems all you care about is what you want to do!" The volume of her voice had lowered but the tone was deadly. She then turned and went into their bedroom, slamming and locking the door behind her.

The rest of the evening was spent in cold silence. Even the boys were quiet, sensing the tension between their parents.

After the boys had gone to bed Vivienne went back into their bedroom and again he heard the door lock. In a few minutes she opened the door and tossed out a pillow and a quilt.

I guess that's a hint I won't be sleeping in our bed tonight, Diego thought as he picked up the bedding and proceeded to make a bed for himself on the sitting room couch. It was the first time they had ever gone to bed angry with each other.

Chapter 18

"What are you doing?" Diego asked the next morning as he watched Vivienne throwing clothes into a suitcase.

"Packing!"

"Where are you going?"

"I'm taking our sons and going back home! I'm not staying somewhere they can be kidnapped and possibly killed," she told him without looking up from what she was doing.

"What happened to Travis could have happened anywhere. Children are taken from their parents, even in San Antonio."

"He wasn't taken in San Antonio. He was in Apache Flats."

"Vivienne! You still aren't thinking rationally. Things can happen to them at Black Creek as well. I can't just pick up and leave."

"Then you stay! I can't take this anymore! I'm taking our babies and leaving this God forsaken country and moving back to civilization."

"You mean you're leaving me and moving back to the ranch?" Diego asked shocked.

"I think I made it very clear, last night, how I feel about living here. If the Rangers mean more to you than your family, I guess I am. The choice is yours."

Suddenly Diego's voice changed from concerned and hurt to the low deliberate tone she had only heard him use when he was about to lose his temper. It was the first time he had ever directed the tone at her.

"You knew the dangers before you accepted my marriage proposal. You said you could live with them."

She stood with her back ramrod straight; then turned, looked him in the eyes and said, "That was before our son was threatened. As I said, the choice is yours. The boys and I are catching the afternoon stage to San Antonio."

"Like hell, you are!" Diego retorted. "Your home is here with me. You're staying right here, where you belong, and we're going to talk about this."

"Like hell, I am!" she snapped,. She whirled and went into Travis' bedroom and began packing his clothes, leaving Diego standing in the hall staring at her back in disbelief. She had never talked to him or anyone else like that before.

After she packed a suitcase for Travis, she went to Charlie Joe's room, expecting the boys to be there. To her shock, the room was empty. With a sense of dread she went to the back door and looked outside. Relieved, she saw them quietly tossing a ball back and forth between them. She wondered how much they had heard of her and Diego's arguments and what they were thinking.

"Travis, Charlie Joe, since school's out we're going to catch the stage in a little while and take a trip to Black Creek to visit your grandparents. While I finish packing come back in the house and tell your father good-bye," she said as calmly as she could manage.

"Papa, aren't you going with us?" Travis asked, when they came inside.

Damn, what am I suppose to say? I don't know the answer to that question myself, Diego thought.

"I'll be along later. This way you'll be able to have a nice long visit. You both behave yourselves. I don't want to get any reports that you've given your mother any trouble. I'm gonna' miss you," he said. He knelt down and gave each of them a hug.

When the stage stopped in San Antonio, a week after leaving

Apache Flats, Vivienne helped the boys to the ground, then looked around. After inquiring about the location of the nearest livery stable they walked there and she rented a horse and buggy. They went back to the stage stop and retrieved their suitcases. She then turned the buggy toward Black Creek.

When they had first left Apache Flats the boys had both asked when Papa was going to join them. Not wanting to lie to them, Vivienne had told them she wasn't sure. However, in a few days they would see both their grandmas and grandpas and all their cousins and of course their ponies. That bit of information seemed to have satisfied them.

The hardest moment had come when Travis asked if the reason they had left without Papa was because of him. That question made her realize the boys had heard more of her and Diego's arguments than she had suspected. After careful thought, she told Travis she had been thinking for a long time about going to Black Creek for a visit. She told them she knew how much they had enjoyed their visit there last summer and thought a visit would keep them from getting bored before school started. She justified her less than truthful response as not wanting Travis to think it was his fault they had left without Diego.

They had just gotten onto Black Creek ranch when Vivienne saw her father riding toward them. He was the last person she wanted to see at this time. She knew he would not understand her coming unannounced and without Diego.

Jace rode up to the wagon and gave them a rather curt greeting. He said, "We didn't know you were coming. Where is Diego?"

"Travis, Charlie Joe, you remember your Grandpa Jace?" she asked the boys. She tried to be cheerful and ignore the dark look her father was giving her.

"Hi Grandpa," they both said, flashing big smiles.

"Diego will be here later when he can get away for a while," Vivienne told her father, repeating what she had heard Diego tell the boys before they left Apache Flats.

After tying his horse to the back of the buggy, Jace got in and without a word took the reins from her.

"I don't want to have to go through this but once. I'll tell you and Mama at the same time," she said quietly.

"Suit yourself," he said.

"Your mother's going to be glad to see you," Jace said after a time.

What about you? Vivienne thought as she looked at him and saw the dark look was still on his face.

"I'll be glad to see her too," Vivienne told him. At the moment she wasn't glad to see him and, the way he was acting, she wasn't about to tell him otherwise.

"As soon as I get you to your house on the ranch, I'll get your mother. I'm assuming that's where you want to go."

"Yes, it is," she answered.

"I'll take the buggy back to San Antonio in the morning."

"Thank you."

The rest of the trip was spent in silence. Even the boys seemed to be intimidated by the atmosphere and didn't say anything.

When the buggy came to a stop in front of the little house where they had lived before moving to Apache Flats, Vivienne saw Maria in the yard hanging up the laundry. Her mother-in-law came up to the buggy and gave them a warm, friendly smile.

"It's good to see you, Vivienne, and my two handsome grandsons. We weren't expecting you," Maria said as she gave Charlie Joe and Travis a hug and helped Vivienne from the buggy.

Jace got out of the buggy, put the suitcases on the ground, and without a word, got back in the buggy and turned it toward his and Amber's house.

You bastard! Maria thought as they watched him drive off. *Vivienne doesn't need your cold silence now. Don't you understand something is seriously wrong for her and the boys to arrive unannounced without Diego?*

After they put the boys down for a nap the two women went into the front room and sat down on the settee.

"I'm not sure if or when Diego is coming," Vivienne said quietly.

"I figured that," Maria said. "Did the two of you have a quarrel?"

"Sort of. Papa has gone to get Mama. When they get here, I'll tell you all about it. Papa is furious with me."

"I don't think he's really angry; he just doesn't understand. But, don't worry, your mother will and she'll be able to reason with your father and help him come to terms with whatever brought you here."

"For the boys sake, I hope so."

Maria just looked at her but didn't comment on her remark.

"Vivienne, I once told you I would fully understand if you had a problem with Diego. I don't need to know what the problem is for you to be welcome here. This will always be your home. You have my love and understanding."

"Oh, thank you," Vivienne said. "But it's not Diego. It's me," she managed to say before bursting into tears.

"It's going to be all right," Maria said. She took Vivienne in her arms and comforted her.

There was a quiet knock at the door. Maria rose and went to the door. She wasn't surprised to see Seth standing there. He seemed to always know when something unexpected happened on the ranch.

"I just saw Jace. He said Vivienne had come back with the children and Diego wasn't with them. What happened?" he asked.

"I don't know. All Vivienne has said so far, is she and Diego had an argument. Jace has gone to get Amber. When they get here, Vivienne is going to tell us what happened," Maria said quietly.

It wasn't long until there was another knock on the door.

When Seth opened it, Amber came rushing in. Jace wasn't far behind.

"Oh, Mama!" Vivienne said. She collapsed tearfully, into her mother's arms. The others exchanged questioning looks. When her sobs finally ceased, she took a deep breath, and collected her thoughts. Pulling away, she told them why she and the boys had come to Black Creek, without Diego.

"Oh, Vivienne, what a difficult decision for you to make!" Amber said when she had finished. "I understand your feelings, but I'm afraid I don't have any suggestions as to what you should do. You're going to need some time to consider everything carefully."

"You married him for better or worse," Jace reprimanded.

At that, Vivienne again burst into tears.

"Mr. Prescott," Amber said, glaring at her husband, "if you can't say something to comfort your daughter then, please, just keep your mouth shut."

"Vivienne, I fully understand why you came back here," Maria told her. "If it's all right with you, I would like to write Diego and try to explain the situation from my point of view."

"Oh, yes! Please do. Try to make him understand I love him but I can't stay somewhere our children aren't safe. When you were visiting us you saw a few of the dangers and problems we face daily."

"Yes, I did. And I understand the pressure those dangers put on you. Seth and I will leave now so you can be with your parents. Just remember, we love you all and we both understand your situation."

As they were leaving the house, Maria cast a quick look toward Jace. She was glad to see the dark look that had been on his face had softened. Apparently Amber's harsh words had done some good.

"This doesn't surprise me in the least." Maria told Seth as they were walking back to their house. "Remember, on the way back from Apache Flats after our visit, I told you about some of the dangers the boys face every day and Vivienne's worries about them. You do understand her situation, don't you?"

"I'd be a fool to say I don't," he answered, remembering the reprimand Amber had given Jace. He knew Maria could be just as tough. He looked at the expression on her face, and added, "Yes, I do understand."

"Hopefully, Diego will come to his senses and realize it too," Maria said. "You don't pull a mother and her babies from their home and family, stick them out in the middle of nowhere and expect her to go through what Vivienne experienced and not do something drastic.

"That part of Texas needs a single man. Not one with a family. You'd think the Rangers would have sense enough to know that.

"Do you think Jace will ever understand why Vivienne had to do what she did?" Maria asked, reflecting back on his actions.

"If anyone can convince him to see it, Amber can. She's one tough lady."

After Amber and Jace had visited with Vivienne awhile Amber said, "I know you're exhausted. Why don't you go take a nap? I'll stay here and watch the boys in case they get up before you do.

"Your father can go back to town. I'm sure Seth will be glad to take me home when I'm ready."

"I'll come get you," Jace said.

"I wouldn't want to put you out," Amber said to him coldly. Vivienne had never heard her mother use that tone of voice.

"It's no bother, I'll tell Maria and Seth I'll be back later to get you," Jace said. He got up and walked out the door.

"Mama, I'm so sorry I'm the cause of you and Papa having words."

"Don't worry about it. I'm not as angry with him as he thinks. Sometimes I just have to exaggerate my feelings in order to make him understand."

"Does Papa know you do that?" Vivienne asked surprised.

"No, and I hope he never does. If he figures that out, I'll lose my advantage," she said, then smiled.

"Now, you go get some rest. If the boys wake up before you do, I'll take them to visit with Maria so they won't disturb you."

"Thank you. I am exhausted," Vivienne said. She got up and gave her mother a hug, then went into the bedroom to get a nap.

Amber had found a rag and was dusting when Travis came into the room, rubbing the sleep from his eyes. "Grandma! Where's Mama?" he asked.

"She's resting. As soon as Charlie Joe wakes up we'll go visit your Grandma Maria. Come sit by me and I'll tell you a story while we wait."

Amber began a story she had heard Maria reading often to her other grandchildren. It was one she was certain Travis had not yet heard. She had just finished when Charlie Joe came into the room.

"Where's Mama?" he asked.

"She's taking a nap."

"I didn't know grownups took naps."

"They do when they're really tired," Amber told him.

"Papa, didn't come with us," Charlie Joe told her.

"But he's coming later," Travis quickly added.

"Yes, I know," Amber said. She didn't know what else she could say to comfort the boys.

"Let's go visit your Grandma Maria and get something to eat."

"Do you think she'll have some cookies?" Travis asked.

"Maybe. But we won't know until we get there."

"Come on, Travis, let's go," Charlie Joe said. He went to where his brother was sitting and began impatiently pulling on his arm.

Chapter 19

A few days later Vivienne and the boys went to visit her mother. While the boys were outside playing, Amber and Vivienne were inside talking.

"Your father finally understands why you came back to Black Creek. But, don't expect him to tell you that. You know how hard it is for him to admit when he's wrong about something."

"I don't care if he never apologizes. I'm just happy he's not still upset with me. And thank you for all you did to help him understand."

After a short silence Amber looked at Vivienne thoughtfully and said, "I understand your situation more than you realize. I'm going to tell you something I've never told anyone, and I don't want you to tell anyone either. Please don't ever say anything to your father about it. He and I have never even mentioned it to each other since it happened.

"Shortly before you were born, I left your father."

"Oh, Mama! I knew you and Papa had some rough times when you were first married, but I had no idea you had ever left him. What happened?"

There was a moment of silence as Amber thought about what she was going to say. Finally, she took a deep breath, looked Vivienne directly in the eye and continued. "I found out he was seeing another woman," she said quietly.

"I did just what you did. I ran away," she added quickly. "Since I didn't have any family to go to, I packed my bags and caught the stage to Ysleta. I didn't tell your father where I was going, or when or if I was coming back. I needed time away from him to think and I didn't want him following me. Of course, I knew if he really wanted to find me he could. But I was hoping he had enough respect for my desire to be alone that he wouldn't do that."

"What made you decide to go back to him?"

"While I was in Ysleta I met a very wise *senora* who told me, if I truly loved him, I should give him a second chance. She also told me to let him know, in no uncertain terms, if he was unfaithful ever again, I would leave for good and would not come back.

"After talking to her, I soon realized she was right and he did deserve a second chance. She also hinted that I might be with child. I hadn't realized that possibility because I was so busy thinking about your father and how much I loved him and missed him. She was right about that too. I knew I didn't want our child to grow up without Jace. I promised myself I would do all I could to make our marriage work and to have a happy home life for our baby, for you.

"The hard part was when I went back to Wolf Creek and saw your father. I had to keep reminding myself I had to be firm when I told him I would not give him another chance.

"Coming back was the best thing I ever did. I think the separation made us both realize how much we love each other and how much our marriage means to us."

"I'm so glad you gave Papa that second chance. I know he's not always easy to live with, but I love him very much. I can't imagine my life without him."

"I can't imagine life without him either," Amber smiled.

"Our son must be doing some deep thinking," Seth said to Maria one evening after Vivienne had taken the boys home to put them to bed. "Vivienne and the boys have been here more than two weeks and she hasn't heard from him. He hasn't even answered the letter you wrote."

"He needs to do some deep thinking!"

"You're not ever going to see his side are you?" he asked.

"Oh, I see his side! When he accepted that assignment to Apache Flats, he wasn't thinking about his family. He was only thinking about himself and what he wanted to do."

"Vivienne agreed to go with him when he told her he had been assigned to Apache Flats. She didn't have any objections to the move," Seth said.

"Believe me, she had reservations about moving there. But, what choice did she have? She loves Diego and she didn't realize at the time just how remote and hostile that part of the state is."

"Maybe Diego didn't realize how dangerous it was out there. Since it was his first assignment, he might have been reluctant to refuse," Seth responded, trying to defend their son's decision.

"He knew the dangers! That's why he was so eager to go. You know danger has always intrigued him. And since when has he been reluctant to stand up for himself? I'll be willing to bet he had no objections when he was told that's where he would be going."

"I think we'd better change the subject before we get into an argument about this," Seth said when he saw the look on her face.

"I think that's an excellent idea.

"Amber and I are going to take Vivienne and the boys to San Antonio Thursday to do some early Christmas shopping before school starts. I know you hate to shop, but do you want to go with us?"

"If I say no, who's going to drive you?"

"I'll ask one of the men to take us."

"You know I don't like you going all that way without me. I can find something to do while the rest of you shop," he said, somewhat reluctantly.

"Are you sure? We don't want to be any trouble for you."

"Can we forget our little disagreement? I don't like it when we're at odds with each other."

"Well, I guess I can forgive you. If you can forgive me." A smile slowly crossed her face as he pulled her close.

Thursday, as they were driving into San Antonio, Maria noticed both boys were being exceptionally quiet. She knew it was because they were unhappy about spending the day shopping.

"What are those funny looking things on the ground?" Travis asked, as he looked out the window of the coach.

"Those are the railroad tracks that the train goes on," Seth told him.

"Where's the train?" Charlie Joe asked.

"It's somewhere between Galveston and Austin."

"I want to ride the train!" Charlie Joe said.

"We don't have anywhere to go on the train," his mother said.

"We could go see Papa," Travis suggested hopefully.

"The train doesn't go to Apache Flats," his mother flatly responded.

"I don't care! I want to ride on the train!" Charlie Joe insisted.

"We're not going on the train so you can forget that idea. And I don't want to hear anymore about it!" Vivienne said, sternly.

At her words Charlie Joe pressed his lips firmly together and squinted his eyes.

You may look like your mother but you definitely have your father's temper, Maria thought, as she looked at the expression on her grandson's face.

When they got to their rooms at the hotel and Maria and Seth were alone, she asked if he would take the boys to the train station that afternoon while she and Vivienne did their shopping. "They can at least see the station and maybe the train will come by while you're there. I know all of you will enjoy that much more than shopping. While you're there could you discreetly get the train's schedule to Austin? I would like to take the boys for a train ride sometime soon.

"Don't say anything to Vivienne or the boys just yet. I would like for it to be a surprise for them."

"I know they'll both be thrilled to do that," Seth replied somewhat wistfully.

After Maria and Vivienne had finished their shopping, they went back to the hotel to get ready for supper. Just as they were about to walk up the stairs to their rooms, Seth and the boys came into the lobby.

"We got to see the train station and meet one of the men who drive the train," Charlie Joe yelled, as he ran across the lobby to where they were.

"Well, you had a good day after all," Amber said with a smile.

"Did you get all your shopping done?" Seth asked as they walked up the stairs to their rooms.

"Most of it. I even got something for you. And don't go looking through my packages when I'm not around. I gave it to Vivienne to keep until Christmas." She knew his curiosity was as strong as the grandchildrens'.

"Did you get the train schedule for me?" Maria asked Seth when they were in their room.

"Yes," he said. He pulled the schedule out of his pocket and handed it to her.

"Oh good. She paused to look it over. "They have a train leaving here every Friday afternoon that gets to Austin that evening. Can you bring us to San Antonio next Thursday? Of course, since school starts Monday Vivienne will need to talk to Mr. Jamison to find out if it's all right for the boys to miss two days of school."

"Are you planning to take the whole family?" he asked.

"No. I just want to take Vivienne and the boys. Hopefully, a train ride will help take their minds off Diego for a little while."

"Good. I don't think I can afford to take the whole family. You know if we take Travis and Charlie Joe, the rest of the grandchildren will want to go too."

"I thought about that. I guess we'll eventually take all of them. Do you want to go with us?" she asked.

"You know I do! I've never ridden a train."

"You'll probably enjoy it as much as the boys will."

"Probably," he admitted.

The next day, Seth took Travis, Charlie Joe and Matthew for a ride to Miguel and Lila's so they could play with Daniel. After they left, Maria told Vivienne about her idea to take the boys for a train ride.

"Oh, they'll love that! They have been after me to take them ever since we got back from San Antonio and they saw the train station."

"If you don't want to go, Seth and I can take the boys. You might want some time away from the responsibility of the boys for a couple of days to think about things."

"I can't imagine life without them for two days. But, I would like to give it a try. If you're certain they won't be too much trouble for you."

"We will enjoy them. If they should get out of line, I'm sure the words and looks Seth used on Diego and Antonio that worked so well when they were that age, will work just as well on Travis and Charlie Joe."

When Seth came in for supper that evening he had a broad smile on his face.

"I'm glad to see you survived your ride with your four grandsons," Maria said.

"I'm proud to say they're all good little horsemen. Charlie Joe, in particular. He has a way with horses that I've only seen in Diego and Cody. He's well on his way to being as good a rider as Diego. It won't be long before he'll be needing a larger and more spirited mount."

"That's because, like you and Diego, he's fearless. Just because he is a good rider, I hope you didn't take your eyes off of him," Maria said.

"I never take my eyes off that little rascal," he laughed. "You never know what he might do next. As you said, he's not afraid of anything."

The day before they were to leave and Vivienne told the boys they were going to San Antonio neither of them were happy. They wanted to know why they had to go.

"Because Grandma and Grandpa are going and they want you to go with them. I think they might have a surprise for you."

"What's the surprise?" Charlie Joe asked excitedly.

"It wouldn't be a surprise if I told you," Vivienne said.

"Are you going?" Travis asked.

"No. I thought you'd enjoy the trip more if it's just you and your grandparents. I want you to behave yourselves and do everything they tell you."

"We will," Charlie Joe said solemnly. "Papa said if you do something Grandpa Seth doesn't like, he whips hard."

"I'm sure he does and, if you're tempted to do something you know you shouldn't, just remember that."

"You can trust us to be good, Mama. Papa told us a man always stands by his word!" Travis told her.

At her son's words tears welled up in Vivienne's eyes.

"Did I say something wrong?" Travis asked. "I didn't mean to make you cry."

"No. I'm just proud of you for remembering that," Vivienne said. She smiled and blinked back her tears.

When Diego opened his post office box and saw a letter, he

hoped it was from Vivienne. He picked the letter up and had to grin. He could barely read the handwriting but he did make out, Texas Ranger, Diego Black, Apache Flats, Texas. This could only be from Charlie Joe. *He's well on his way to having my illegible handwriting,* he thought with a grin as he opened it.

"Dear Papa," he read. "I miss you. When are you cumin to Black Creek? Pleze git my whissle and give it to Katrina. Tel her I mis her. Luv, Charlie Joe."

It appears he's also going to be as bad a speller as I am. This separation is hell on all of us. Now for the task of finding that whistle in Charlie Joe's room. There's no telling where he's hidden it. I'm surprised he's willing to give it up for any reason. To him that is a very valuable possession. I hope Katrina appreciates the supreme sacrifice he's making to give it to her.

With that, he went through the General Store and told Joaquin and Teresa good-bye. Then headed to the house to find the whistle and to write Charlie Joe. He wanted to let him know he had received the letter and followed his instructions. *I wonder if Katrina misses Charlie Joe?* he thought.

CHAPTER 20

During breakfast at the hotel the next morning, the boys asked when they were going to get to go home. Suppressing a smile at the forlorn expressions on their faces, Maria looked at them and said, "Not until Sunday."

At her words both boys let out a loud groan. "What are we going to do until then?" Travis asked.

"Don't worry," Maria told them, "I'm sure we can find something for you to do that you'll enjoy."

"Mama said you have a surprise for us. What is it?" Charlie Joe asked.

"If we do have a surprise for you I'm not going to tell you until it's time. No matter how hard you plead," Maria said, then smiled.

Later that morning, when they pulled up to the train depot and stopped, Travis looked at Seth and asked hopefully, "Are we going to get to ride the train?"

"Is that our surprise?" Charlie Joe asked.

When Seth told them they were going to get to ride the train, both boys let out a loud "Whoopee!" and jumped out of the buggy.

"Where's the train?" Charlie Joe asked.

"It'll be here directly," Seth told him. "We got here a little early to be sure we didn't miss it."

Seth put the horses and buggy in the stable, then went back to the depot to wait with the family. It wasn't long until they heard a loud whistle. Before either of the boys could ask if that was the train, they saw a plume of black smoke and the train appeared from around a curve.

"It's so big!" Charlie Joe said in amazement.

"And so loud," Travis said. He put his hands over his ears as the train came to a loud screeching stop, not far from where they stood.

After the platform was lowered so the arriving passengers could get off, the family went to the platform and showed their tickets.

Just as Seth was about to help Maria onto the train they heard the conductor call out in a loud voice that could be heard over all the noise, "All Abo-o-oard."

"What does that mean?" Travis asked.

"He's telling us it's time for everyone to get on the train," Seth answered. He then helped Maria onto the platform and lifted the boys up then got on himself.

"Now sit down and be still," Maria told them when they found four vacant seats.

"I want to look around," Charlie Joe said.

"We're going to have to stay in our seats for a while. The train is going to start moving shortly. Maybe later, when it stops to pick up more passengers, we can look around," Seth told them.

About that time they heard the whistle blow. Suddenly, the train lurched forward and started slowly moving. Both boys had their faces pressed against the window pane looking out. When they got out of town, the train picked up speed.

"It's going so fast!" Travis said in amazement.

"It's traveling about thirty miles an hour. It will be going at this speed all the way to Austin. We're scheduled to get there about five o'clock this evening," Seth told them.

"Wow! That's a lot quicker than a horse can get there," Travis said.

"That it is," Seth answered.

"What makes it go so fast?" Travis asked.

"It's powered by steam."

"How does steam make it go?" Travis asked.

"Later, when we look around, maybe we'll see the engineer and you can ask him."

"What's the matter, dear? Don't tell me you don't know how a steam engine works," Maria quietly teased.

Seth didn't say anything. He just gave her a quick look, then turned his attention back to the boys.

When the train stopped in San Marcos to take on more passengers, Seth took the boys for a look around. Just as the train started up again, Charlie Joe and Travis came running down the aisle yelling, "We saw the engine room and got to meet the engineer. He told us how steam makes the train run."

The boys were looking out the window talking about the train when Travis suddenly shouted, "Look! Buffalo!"

They all to where Travis was pointing and saw there was indeed a small herd of buffalo. "Consider yourselves very fortunate," Seth told them. "There aren't many of those left in this area."

"They're so ugly! Were there a lot of them here when you first came to Texas?" Travis asked.

"Yes. Way back then there were millions of them. I saw a herd nearly every day," he told his grandson.

Maria had a hard time keeping a straight face over his exaggerated number of buffalo that had been in the area a mere forty years ago.

When they arrived in Austin the boys took a long look around the depot. They asked questions the entire time until they were finally convinced they had seen everything.

When they checked into the hotel, the desk clerk told

them if they wanted to eat in the dining room they had best hurry. It would only be open another thirty minutes.

"Are you ready to go to our rooms and rest?" Maria asked hopefully, as they were finishing supper.

Travis and Charlie Joe both answered with an emphatic, "No!"

"The capitol building isn't far from here," Seth told them. "We can go see that before it gets dark."

"The three of you can go without me. I think I'll go to the room and rest," Maria said.

"What are we going to do tomorrow?" Travis asked his grandfather, as they were walking up the avenue toward the Capitol building.

"We won't have much time to sightsee. The train leaves here at two o'clock. I thought we might go look at Barton Springs Creek. I've heard it's something anyone who comes to Austin must see," Seth told them.

"Is it prettier than the creek on Black Creek?" Charlie Joe asked.

"I've never seen it, but I've heard it is. It's supposedly deeper and bigger."

After breakfast the next morning Maria went to the hotel desk and asked if they would pack a lunch for the family, so they could have a picnic by the creek.

After getting the lunch basket, they rented a buggy and headed for Barton Springs. A few minutes after crossing the Colorado River, they reached their destination.

"Oh, Seth, this is beautiful. The water is so clear," Maria said. She had found them a shady spot on the hillside overlooking the creek to spread their quilt.

"Grandma, can we go swimming?" Travis asked.

"We didn't bring anything for you to wear to go swimming.

But if you take off your shoes and stockings and roll up your pant legs, you can wade in the water."

"I'll go with them. You can stay here and enjoy the scenery," Seth told her.

"Thank you. You'd better be quick, they already have their shoes off," she said.

This is really beautiful, she thought as she looked around at the overhanging cliffs and the beautiful large oak trees. Her imagination was working overtime as she imagined what good hiding places the cliffs must have provided the Indians not so long ago. Still thinking about the Indians, she jumped when she heard the boys let out a loud squeal. For a moment she thought they had stepped on something and hurt themselves.

Then she heard Seth laugh and ask, "Did I forget to mention how cold the water is?"

"Why is it so cold?" Travis asked.

"I don't know. I just know it's cold all year no matter how hot the weather is."

"Does it freeze in the winter?"

"No. The water flows too fast for that to happen."

They slowly got accustomed to the cold water, waded in up to their knees and began splashing each other. *It's a good thing it's a warm day,* Maria thought as she watched them. *They might not be swimming but they're going to be soaked by the time they stop for lunch.*

About that time, Charlie Joe came running up the hill with something in his hand. "Look what I found," he said, thrusting the thing toward her. "Grandpa said it's a crawfish. He said if you get enough of them you can throw them in a pot of boiling water and cook them and then eat them."

"That's very interesting but watch out for those pinchers. They could give you a bad nip," Maria warned, as she tried not to look too closely at the ugly little creature.

"I've got to go put it back in the water before it dies," he said. He turned and ran back down the hill toward the water.

She watched them a little longer, keeping a close eye on

the time, before calling them for lunch.

"This is a lot more fun than seeing the 'ole Capitol building," Charlie Joe said. He sat down on the quilt and grabbed a piece of chicken and started eating.

When they finished their picnic, Maria began picking up the dirty dishes and putting them in the basket to take back to the hotel.

As they were walking back to the buggy, Seth heard Maria let out a quiet gasp. "What's wrong?" he asked, concerned.

"Don't turn or say anything but one of the women in that group of people over there is Darrell's mother," she said quietly. "Let's get away from here. I certainly don't want to have a confrontation with that woman. I'm sure she still blames us for Darrell and her husband going to prison. I'm thankful Noelle isn't with us."

"Don't you think by now she's realized someone would have discovered it was Darrell and his father who were instrumental in the attempted assassination of the governor? We might have been responsible for them getting caught sooner than they otherwise would have, but eventually, they would have been found out."

"No. She's too dumb to figure that out."

"Are you sure it's her?"

"Without a doubt. She looks twenty years older than she did the last time I saw her, but it's definitely her." With that they hurried toward the buggy.

"Are you ready for the train ride home?" Seth asked the boys later, as they were headed to the train station for the trip home. When they answered with a quiet, "Yes sir," Maria looked at them and knew they would both be sleeping all the way back. It had been a busy and exciting two days for them.

Vivienne was lying in bed listening to the patter of rain against the window. She wondered if this early cold snap was an indication it was going to be a long, cold winter. Her thoughts were interrupted by a knock at the door. Who could that be at this hour of the night and in this weather? she asked herself as she got out of bed and reached for her robe.

When she opened the door a blast of cold air and rain hit her and she saw Diego standing there. All he said to her stunned silence was, "I love you."

"Oh, Diego, I love you too!" she said. He came into the house and shut the door behind him.

"I've missed you," she said, as she went into his arms.

He drew her close then slowly turned and gently pressed her against the door. She could feel his hardened shaft press against her as they kissed. She knew he wanted her as much as she wanted him.

"I love you," he said, as he ran kisses down her neck. "I need you." Still kissing her, he picked her up and carried her into the bedroom.

After he laid her down on the bed she quickly slipped out of her robe and gown and he hurriedly removed his wet clothes. As he undressed, her eyes never left him. "I want you," she said.

He turned and looked at her. "I want you too," he said. As he laid down on the bed his kisses made a trail down her body until he reached her toes.

"I've never had my toes kissed," she said.

"Did you like it?" he asked.

"Yes, but not as much as what you're about to do," she said. She felt his shaft enter her waiting body.

After they made love they lay there quietly holding each other for several minutes before Diego broke the silence.

"I've been doing a lot of thinking about you and what happened. I've come to realize you were right. And, I've made some decisions about our future that we need to talk about," he said. He propped himself up on his elbow and gently stroked her cheek.

"I sold the house in Apache Flats and all but the three horses I brought with me today. I'm planning to go to Ranger Headquarters and ask them to transfer me to another district.

"If they won't do that, I'll resign from the Rangers and ask Jace if he can take me on as his deputy Marshal. If he can't do that, I'll stay on Black Creek and work with Papa and my brothers."

"Oh, Diego! Would you really do that?"

"Yes. As you told me before you left, the choice is mine. I enjoy being a Ranger but you and the boys mean more to me than they ever will. We'll stay here until I find out where I'll be going.

"Captain Jones and I went on a case a couple of weeks ago. I told him you had come back here and that I was willing to give up being a Ranger for you and the boys. He didn't seem the least bit surprised about anything I said. He thinks very highly of you. He said to give you his best."

"I think very highly of him also. I'm going to miss him. He is truly a nice man. He and Joaquin and Teresa are all I'm going to miss about Apache Flats. Of course, I'll miss Rafael and Lapopa as well," she added with a grin.

At the mention of Lapopa's name, Diego didn't say anything. He just looked at her and shook his head in amazement.

"What about all our clothes and the furnishings in the house in Apache Flats?" Vivienne asked.

"That's all been taken care of. Before I left I packed everything and arranged for it to be sent here. It should all be arriving within the week."

"You packed everything?" Vivienne asked, suppressing a laugh. "I didn't know you knew how to do that."

"What's so hard about putting things in a trunk?" he asked in all innocence.

"Not a thing. Thank you for doing that so I don't have to

go back out there." She could only imagine the condition their things would be in when they arrived.

"The boys are going to be thrilled to see you. They've missed you so much."

"I've missed the little rascals also. It's too quiet and boring without them around."

CHAPTER 21

"I never thought a little cold rain would send you back inside," Maria said the next morning when Seth came back into the house, just minutes after leaving.

"I thought you might like to know there are three horses in the barn that weren't there last night. One of them has the Black Creek brand on him."

"Do you think it's Diego?" she asked hopefully.

"That's my guess."

"Well, if it is, it certainly took him long enough to come to his senses."

"Don't forget, she's the one who left him," Seth reminded her.

"And don't you forget the reason she left," Maria responded testily.

"You women will always stick up for each other, won't you?" he asked, shaking his head.

"We only stick up for each other when we're right."

"Are you ever wrong?"

"Very seldom," she said with a smile.

"Shall we go to their house and see if it is Diego?" he asked.

"No. Let him come here after he and Vivienne have had some time together to talk."

"If it is him, I doubt it's just talk that's on their minds. In case it is Diego, I'm going to stick around for awhile. I don't want to miss him."

The words were hardly out of his mouth when the kitchen door flew open and Travis and Charlie Joe came running in. Diego and Vivienne were close behind them.

"Papa's home!" the boys yelled excitedly at the same time.

"It's good to see you, son," Seth said. He stood and extended his hand to Diego.

"Oh Seth, don't be so formal," Maria said. She threw her arms around Diego and gave him a hug. "We've missed you."

"I've missed all of you too," Diego said, then smiled.

"Are you here to stay?" Seth asked.

"I'm not sure. All I know is I won't be going back to Apache Flats." He looked at Vivienne and smiled.

"Vivienne and I've been talking. I'm going into San Antonio this morning to Ranger Headquarters and talk to them about being assigned to another district. If they don't agree to transfer me, I guess Black Creek will have another *vaquero*."

Maria didn't say anything. As she looked at Vivienne, Vivienne met her gaze and raised her eyebrows. She knew Diego was hoping they would assign him to another district. It was obvious Vivienne, like herself, was hoping the Rangers would turn his request down and they would be staying at Black Creek.

"Have ya'll had breakfast?" Maria asked.

"No, ma'am," Diego responded.

"Well, you're not going anywhere until you do," she said.

"I'm hungry too!" Charlie Joe said.

"I thought I'd fix breakfast for all of you," she said, smiling at her grandsons.

"I want hotcakes," Travis said.

"I want scrambled eggs," Charlie Joe quickly added.

"Can the two of you ever agree on anything?" Maria laughed. "Today the choice is your father's. What would you like, Diego?"

"Scrambled eggs and hotcakes. Along with some bacon and potatoes," he answered with a big grin.

"I see your appetite hasn't decreased," she laughed.

"I'll make the eggs and bacon and potatoes, while you

make the hotcakes," Vivienne told her. "I know everyone likes your hotcakes better than mine."

"That comes from making them for four hungry men for thirty years," Maria told her.

When breakfast was on the table, Maria saw Seth pick up a plate and scoop some eggs on it. "Mr. Black, I believe you've already had breakfast," she admonished.

"How about fixing me a couple of pieces of toast? If I'm going into San Antonio with Diego, I'll need all the energy I can get. We won't get back home until tomorrow."

"I'll be glad to fix you some toast," Vivienne told him. "Would anyone else like some?" No one else said they wanted any but knowing the men in the family she fixed several extra pieces anyway, knowing they would be eaten.

"I didn't know you had plans to go to San Antonio today," Maria said with a smile. "Vivienne might want to go with Diego."

"Oh. I didn't think about that," he said, looking at Vivienne.

"No, thank you. In this kind of weather, I only make that trip when I absolutely have to. Now that Diego is back home, I'll let him go without me."

"I wanna' go," Travis piped up.

"Me too!" Charlie Joe said.

How much their wishes have changed in just a few weeks, Maria thought with a smile. *The last time we told them we were going to San Antonio they were both miserable at the thought.*

"Not this time, boys. Today you're going to stay home and help Grandma and Mama eat an apple pie," Maria told them.

"And don't forget today is a school day," Vivienne reminded them.

"Since Papa's home, do we have to go to school?" Charlie Joe asked.

"I think you know the answer to that question," Vivienne said. She looked at her son and shook her head.

"That sounds like something Diego would have asked

when he was eight years old," Maria laughed.

"He gets more like his father every day," Vivienne told them. She rolled her eyes and looking at Diego.

"An apple pie?" Seth inquired.

"Don't worry, dear. I'll make two pies so you and Diego can have your share when you get back.

"Some little boys never grow up," she said, looking at Vivienne.

Maria and Vivienne both knew, as soon as Diego and Seth walked into the room the next afternoon, Diego had received the news he wanted from Ranger Headquarters. Seth even seemed pleased.

"Well, sweetheart," Diego said as he sat down next to Vivienne and put his arm around her, "it looks like we're going to be moving to Houston. I've been re-assigned to that district."

Maria noticed Diego was so happy about his news he didn't seem aware of the look of disappointment that flashed across Vivienne's face when he said he had been granted the transfer.

"That's much better than Apache Flats!" Vivienne said. "The area isn't hostile and it's closer to here."

"No one at Ranger headquarters seemed surprised he was there asking for a transfer out of the Apache Flats district. As far as anyone at headquarters can remember, Diego's three years there seems to have set a record. No one has ever stayed that long," Seth told them.

The next day was again cold and wet. So they all stayed home. Miguel and Lila and Daniel came for a visit.

"It's so nice to have all of you here," Maria said, as she looked around the room at the family. "This is the first time we've all been together in such a long time. Lila did you bring a change of clothes for the three of you, so you can spend the night?"

"Yes ma'am. I did."

"Good. The boys can all stay in Victoria's old room and you and Miguel can stay in his old room. Matthew, do you want to stay here with them? I think the bed is big enough to comfortably sleep all you boys."

"Mama, can I please stay?" Matthew asked, looking at Victoria.

"Yes, if you promise to behave yourself."

"I promise!"

"Selena, if you want to stay for the night you can sleep in the nursery," Maria said, suppressing a smile. She knew what her granddaughter's response would be.

"No! I don't want to stay in the same house with these four monsters any longer than I have to."

"Selena! That wasn't a very nice thing to say about your brother and cousins," Victoria said, gently chastising her daughter.

"Well, they are monsters."

"And you're a prissy pest," Matthew told her.

"All right, "Cody said. "I think it's time for everyone age ten and younger to find something to do besides argue."

"Grandma, can I work on that surprise I'm making Mama for Christmas?" Selena asked quietly.

"Of course dear. I'll get it for you and you can work on it in the nursery."

"You boys stay out of the nursery or you'll have me to answer to," Diego said firmly to the four boys. "I want to hear each of you say 'yes, sir,'" he added. After getting a yes sir from them, they all left the room.

"I didn't know my little brother could be such a disciplinarian," Miguel said, grinning.

"He's learned to be since he has two sons and one of them is just like him," Vivienne laughed.

"What goes around, comes around," Miguel laughed.

After supper, they all gathered in the library. Daniel asked, "Grandpa, when you first came to Texas did you have to fight the Indians?"

"No. For the most part the Indians around here were peaceful by that time. The only problem we had with them was, occasionally, they would take a few cattle to feed their people when their hunters couldn't kill enough wildlife to survive."

"Did you let them do that?" Daniel asked, surprised.

"It was either that or start a war with them and no one wanted to do that. There had already been enough fighting and killing," Seth told him.

"I do remember one incident when two men passing through the area crossed onto the land the Indians considered theirs."

"Cody, you probably know the story I'm talking about. Since you and Jace are both part Indian do you mind if I tell the story to the boys?"

"Not in the least. I know some of my relatives could be rather violent. The incident was probably even more violent than the paper reported."

"Jace. What about you?"

"It won't bother me. Why do you think I chose to live in the white man's world?"

"If you're going to tell the story I think you are, the ladies and I are going to leave. If the boys have nightmares tonight because of the stories you're going to tell, you can sit up with them," Maria said as they left the room.

"Tell us everything," Matthew said as the four little boys sat down on the floor around their grandfather.

"Well, if my memory serves me right, there were three men who were traveling from San Antonio to Austin. They had been given a map, showing the safest route to travel, where they were least likely to encounter any Indians. As they rode, two of the men were passing a bottle of whiskey back and forth between them. With each swig they were getting braver and more fool hearted. Not long after they left San Antonio, they saw a trail that would save them several hours of travel and decided to go that way instead.

"The third man argued with them, reminding them how dangerous the route would be. The other two just laughed at him. After some arguing they agreed to meet at the hotel in Austin. The two took the short cut and the third man took the trail that had been recommended. "When the third man arrived in Austin he went to the hotel expecting to meet up with his friends. To his surprise they weren't there and no one had seen them. The next day, when they still hadn't shown up he found several men who agreed to go with him to help find them.

As Seth told the story he watched his grandsons very closely and saw their eyes grow wider and wider with excitement as he talked.

"They hadn't gone far when they found his two friends next to a creek. They had been shot with arrows and scalped."

"Was it Barton Springs Creek?" Travis asked.

"I think it was," Seth told him, thoughtfully.

"Oh, boy. We've been there!" Travis said looking at Matthew.

"Did that really happen?" Daniel asked.

"Yes, and that wasn't the only time that happened during the early settling of Texas but that's the only case I know all the details of because it was written up in the San Antonio paper.

"About that same time your grandmother was a young girl. She was living on *Rio Negro Ranchero,* with her parents, in the house where Daniel and his family are now living, when she was kidnapped by some Indian warriors. Fortunately for all of us the Indians who took her weren't that mean. When we trailed them and found their camp we were able to make a trade with them. They let us have your grandmother back for a dozen of her father's horses."

"How old was Grandma when that happened?" Matthew asked.

"She was thirteen," Seth told him.

"Were you scared when you went into the Indian's camp?" Daniel asked.

"No. But, I should have been."

"Was Grandma scared when the Indians took her?" Matthew asked.

"She said she wasn't."

"Wow! She was really brave for a girl," Matthew said.

"Tell us some more wild Indian stories," Daniel said.

"Yeah," his cousins all said in unison.

Uh oh, I'm in trouble now, Seth thought. *I don't know anymore factual stories. I guess, if I'm going to tell anymore tales, I'm going to have to rely on my imagination.* As he got into his next story, he looked at Jace and Cody. They were each grinning at him, thoroughly enjoying the uncomfortable position he was in. They knew the story he was telling had very few, if any, actual facts in it.

CHAPTER 22

"Mama once accused me of being obtuse and I'm afraid she was right," Diego told Vivienne. They had been in Houston several weeks. "I never realized how unhappy you were living in Apache Flats, until we moved here."

"I tried to be happy but there was so much missing in Apache Flats that I needed to make me truly happy. Besides all the dangers out there, I missed not being close to our families. Houston is much better in so many ways."

"I missed our families too," Diego said.

She noticed he still wouldn't admit to the dangers in Apache Flats.

"Even the boys have said they like living here better. Of course they miss the friends they had in Apache Flats, but they have already made many new friends here. Travis said he likes the school better. Charlie Joe would never admit there is anything good about school, but I know even he likes it better. I know he likes the fact he's not in the same room with Travis like he was at the school in Apache Flats.

"I'm glad both of them are smart because they are really having to work to catch up with the rest of their classmates. Both of their teachers told me the boys are about a semester behind the other students in their classes."

"Do you think they'll have trouble catching up?" Diego asked, concerned.

"No. I'm certain by the end of the school year they will both be caught up. At least I know Travis will. Charlie Joe will be also if he'll just apply himself."

"Do you think it would hurt them to miss a day of school?" Diego asked. "I'd like to take them to the docks to let them see the ships and explain some things about world trade to them. I know they would enjoy it and they might even learn something. I'd take them on a Saturday but the docks get a little rough on the weekends."

"The boys would love that. But, I don't know if the school will feel they would learn enough to miss a day of school for it. I'll ask their teachers tomorrow."

The next day when Diego came home Vivienne met him at the door with a smile. "I talked to both of the boys' teachers and they thought a trip to the docks would be a wonderful learning experience for them, under one condition. You take all the children from both classes with you."

"What?!"

"Oh, it won't be that bad." She had to laugh when she saw the look of horror on his face.

"That's a matter of opinion."

"Both teachers said they would go with you to help and, of course, I'll go. I'm sure some of the other parents will also want to go.

"They said they will need to meet with you before they can give their final approval."

"What have I gotten myself into?" Diego laughed and shook his head. "I'll have to do some research on the subject before I'll be ready to take on forty school kids, two teachers and no telling how many parents. Maybe I can get Lieutenant Mitchell to go with us."

"That's funny," Vivienne said with a laugh. "It takes two big, fearless Texas Rangers to take on forty small children."

"I'd rather face forty Apaches on the war path than forty students that age. Tell the teachers I'll come by Thursday afternoon to meet with them."

"Thank you, dear. You won't regret it."

"I'm not so sure about that."

"Are you ready for this?" Vivienne asked as she and Diego drove to the school to get the students for their outing to the ship channel.

"No. But it's too late to back out now."

When they reached the docks, and the students got out of the buggies, Diego looked at them and said, "The captain of one of the ships has kindly offered to let us board his ship so you can see everything up close. I want you to stay close to your teacher and parents. If anyone strays away from the group they will have Lieutenant Mitchell and me to answer to. Is that clear?" After a solemn "yes, sir," from everyone he smiled and said. "All right, let's go."

Vivienne noticed even the little girls seemed to be in awe of the big ship and all the things they saw. After a couple of hours of touring the ship and walking around the docks, it was time to go back to school.

After taking the children back to the school they drove home. On the way home Vivienne asked Diego and Lieutenant Mitchell if the trip had been as bad as they thought it was going to be. They both reluctantly admitted it hadn't been.

"I was surprised at some of the questions the students asked. Some of them were very adult inquiries," Lieutenant Mitchell said.

"I think some of those questions were ones their parents had told them to ask," Vivienne said.

"Your talk was very interesting and informative. Several of the parents told me they thoroughly enjoyed the tour and that they learned a lot. I think you should plan on doing it again next year," Vivienne said.

"Woman, you're crazy." Diego told her.

"I'm inclined to agree with you," Lieutenant Mitchell laughed.

"They also obeyed better than I thought they would," Diego said.

"The way you looked at them when you told them they had better stay close to the teachers was enough to make a grown man obey," Vivienne told him.

"Do you think I was too tough on them?"

"Not in the least. Under the circumstances, I think the parents who came along appreciated your firmness. In case you didn't know it, the two of you have made yourselves heroes in the eyes of forty young students."

"I think you're exaggerating just a bit," Lieutenant Mitchell said.

"She does have a tendency to do that," Diego told him.

"Mama, look what we have," Travis said when he and Charlie Joe came running in the house after school, one cold November afternoon. With that he pulled a tiny little puppy from inside his jacket.

"Where did you get that?" she asked in surprise.

"Johnny Phillips' dog had puppies. He found homes for all of them, except this one. Mr. Phillips said he's the runt of the bunch and nobody wants him and if we don't take him he's going to have to shoot him. Can we please keep him? We named him *Bueno* because we know he's going to be a good dog and not do anything he shouldn't."

"I don't know," Vivienne said. She looked at the pathetic little pup. "Dogs require a lot of care and attention."

"Oh, please," Travis pleaded. "I promise we'll take care of him. You won't even know he's here."

She looked from the pup to her sons pleading faces, took a deep breath and said, "If you promise to feed and water him and see to all his needs, I suppose you may keep him."

"Oh boy! Thank you, Mama. We promise!"

"The first thing you need to do is to take him outside so he can relieve himself, while I find something for him to eat and bowls to put his food and water in. When your father gets home this evening he can build him a dog house."

As they went out the door she heard Charlie Joe quietly say, "I told you if you asked Mama if we could keep him she'd say yes. She can't say no to you."

Those two little schemers! I wondered why Charlie Joe was being so quiet, Vivienne thought. She had to laugh at herself, as she stood at the door and watched the boys playing with the pup.

"I see we have a new member to the family," Diego said when he came into the house that evening carrying *Bueno* in the palm of his hand.

"Outside!" Vivienne said pointing to the door. "I told the boys they could keep him but he was not to come inside for any reason."

"It's too cold for the boys to stay outside much longer. You don't want them getting sick do you? Besides, *Bueno* is just a tiny little puppy who's use to the warmth and companionship of being with his mother and litter mates. It's going to be too cold for him to stay out there all by himself tonight," Diego said. He had a pathetic, pleading look on his face. She looked at her sons, and saw the same expression on their faces.

"Oh, all right, he can stay in the kitchen until the weather warms up, but after that, he's not to come in the house for any reason. Is that clear?"

"Yes, ma'am," all three answered.

That was too easy, she thought as she looked at them. "The first thing you're going to do after supper, Mr. Black, is to build him a box to sleep in."

"Yes, ma'am," Diego said, smiling.

"The three of you are impossible," she said, shaking her head.

"One of the best things about living in Houston is you're not away from home as much as you were when we were in

Apache Flats. You haven't been gone longer than three days at a time since we've been here," Vivienne told Diego one evening when he came home.

"I'm grateful for that. Those days and nights I was away from home for so long were miserable. But, I'll have to admit, I miss the unpredictable things that happened in west Texas. Since we've been here I haven't had one tracking job or chased even one outlaw on horseback. It seems most of my time now is spent doing paperwork."

You also haven't been shot at the entire time we've been here. For that I'm more thankful that you'll ever know, Vivienne thought.

"I found out something I think you'll be pleased to hear," Vivienne told Diego the next evening when he came home. "I went to see Doctor Ballard this morning and he confirmed something I've been suspecting for a couple of weeks. In about six months we're going to have a baby."

"That's the best news I've heard since you told me you were carrying Charlie Joe," Diego said. A smile crossed his face and he gave her a big hug.

"I don't care if it's another boy, but I would kind of like to have a girl this time so I can spoil her," Diego added.

"I'm hoping for a girl too, but not for that reason."

"You want a girl so the two of you can conspire against the boys and me," he laughed.

"I think it's about time. I've been outnumbered three to one for the past nine years.

"If it is a girl this time, do you still want to name her Victoria Noelle?" Vivienne asked.

"If it's all right with you."

"Of course.

"I've already written the letter to my parents, telling them about the baby. I was waiting to mail the letter until I talked to you.

"Why don't you write your parents and tell them? I think

they would really enjoy hearing the news from you. After you write the letter, I'll mail both of them and everyone will know at the same time."

"Have you told the boys?"

"No. I wanted to tell you first."

"You know they're going to be wanting a brother."

"I know. If it is a boy, I'll be outnumbered four to one. Three to one is bad enough," she laughed.

"It looks like we won't be seeing Diego and his family for a while unless we go to Houston," Maria said as she read Diego's letter. "They're going to have another baby."

"I guess I'd better be prepared to make several trips to Houston between now and the time the baby comes. At least the trip will be quicker and more comfortable than the coach ride we made when they lived in Apache Flats. When do you want to make the first trip?" Seth asked.

"Travis, I'm proud of you and Charlie Joe for how well you're taking care of *Bueno*. I haven't had to remind you even once to tend to him," Vivienne told him one morning. He got up from the table and began putting scraps of food in the puppy's dish. "Thanks to your good care, he's growing and his coat is nice and shiny."

"He's fun to take care of," Travis told her.

"Okay, you two, it's time to be off to school," Vivienne said and gave each of them a hug.

"I guess that means it's time for me to go to work. Don't wait supper on me tonight. I probably won't be home until eleven or twelve o'clock," Diego said as he put on his hat and kissed her good-bye.

Before she had a chance to ask why he was going to be so late, he was out the door.

"Sergeant Ames, Lieutenant Mitchell, I know you're both wondering why I asked you to meet me here on the bayou, Diego said that evening when the three rangers met. "The reason is because I didn't want anyone to know we were meeting or to overhear what I'm about to say," Diego told them.

"As you both know, there are several gambling rings here in Houston. One in particular is especially large. The sheriff has been trying to shut down the club where they meet. He and I have gone to the club several times lately but, whenever we get there, all the gaming tables are cleared and the chips and other gambling devices have been stowed somewhere out of sight. The place is suddenly turned into a respectable gentleman's club. My personal feeling is the sheriff has warned them ahead of time that we were coming."

"That's a pretty strong accusation," Sergeant Ames said.

"I know. But my feelings are so strong I won't be able to rest until I know if I'm right. I can't raid it alone. That's why I've called on you. Are you with me?" he asked.

"You bet," Lieutenant Mitchell said. "There's nothing worse than a lawman who's working on the wrong side of the law."

Sergeant Ames nodded his head in agreement.

"Good. Here's what we'll do." Diego then proceeded to tell them his plans for shutting down the gambling casino.

At nine o'clock the three Rangers rode up to the club. As they dismounted, Diego quietly said, "Keep your guns holstered but be prepared to use them at a moment's notice. Some of the men may become hostile at the possibility of being arrested."

As Diego quietly opened the door and walked in the club it looked just as he thought it would. Men were standing around one of the tables shooting craps, a roulette wheel was spinning on another table and the other three tables had men sitting around them playing poker.

"Texas Rangers," Diego said loud enough to be heard over the din in the room. At his words the room suddenly turned deadly quiet as everyone turned and looked at the three Rangers.

Looking around the room Diego saw several prominent men of the city. He wasn't the least surprised to see one of those men was Sheriff Edison.

"We've come to close this place down. Everyone keep your seats except for the dealers and everyone who works in the club and, of course, Sheriff Edison. I want all of you to stand against the wall over there," he said, pointing to the wall adjacent to the bar. "Don't any of you try to slip out of here because, if you do, we'll find you and you'll wish you hadn't sneaked out."

When they had all done as he requested, he told the men seated they were free to leave. "But don't plan to come back here," he told them. "As of now, this place is officially and permanently closed.

"Is there by any chance a wagon around here?" Diego asked. When there was no answer Sergeant Ames said he would see if he could find one.

"While he's gone, Lieutenant Mitchell will you search everyone to see if they have any weapons on them. That includes the ladies, as well as the men."

When the search was completed, there was a large collection of assorted guns and knives on one of the tables.

About that time Lieutenant Mitchell came back into the room and told them he had found a wagon.

"Good. Now if all of you will get in the wagon we'll take you to the jail," Diego told the prisoners. "Mr. Edison, since the wagon is crowded, I'll let you drive it so my partners and I can devote our attention to watching all of you. I believe you know the way."

"Lieutenant Mitchell," Diego said when they reached the jail and all the prisoners were in the cells and the doors were locked, "you can keep the first watch tonight. Sergeant Ames you can go home and get some sleep. Be back here at ten o'clock in the morning to relieve the lieutenant. After I tell the mayor about what has transpired, I'll go home and get a little shut eye. I'll be back later to start the legal process for the arrest of these prisoners."

More damn paper work, Diego thought. *I wonder how long it will take some judge to dismiss the charges against Sheriff Edison. Even at that his reputation as a law officer around here will be ruined. As desperate as they are for lawmen in El Paso County they would probably hire him out there. I may recommend him for a position in Presidio.* The thought of Sheriff Edison in the rugged and socially deprived western part of the state, away from the luxuries he was accustomed to in Houston, brought a smile to his face.

CHAPTER 23

Grace Phillips had come over for Vivienne to help her make some new curtains for the Phillips' sitting room. While the women worked on the curtains, Travis and Johnny were outside playing with *Bueno.*

"I've been meaning to ask you, did Brad really tell Travis and Charlie Joe he was going to have to shoot *Bueno* if they didn't take him?"

"Is that what they told you? I think your boys' imagination might have been working a little overtime if they said that," Grace laughed. "I believe what Brad actually said was he didn't know what he was going to do with the pup if they didn't take him."

"I thought it was probably something like that. I'm sure they knew if they didn't exaggerate on what Brad had told them, I wouldn't let them keep the pup."

About that time Travis came into the room with a request. "Mama, Johnny said there's an old voodoo woman who lives not far from here on the bayou. Can we go see her?"

"No. It's too dangerous in the bayou for the two of you alone."

"Will you take us?"

"No. Maybe, when your father comes home, he'll take you."

"When's he coming home?"

"Monday or Tuesday."

"But, we'll be in school then," he said. He gave her a

pitiful look at the thought of the long wait.

"I'm sorry," Vivienne replied, "but you aren't going unless he's with you."

"Tell Johnny I'm in complete agreement with your mother about the two of you going," Grace told him.

"Well, what did she say?" Johnny asked when Travis came back outside.

"She said we couldn't go unless Papa took us and he won't be able to take us until Saturday."

"That's too long to wait," Johnny added. "It's not far from here. We could go and be back before anyone knows we're gone."

When Travis didn't say anything, Johnny said, "I'll bet she knows that famous voodoo lady, Marie Laveau, who lives in New Orleans. We can ask her if she does. Maybe she'll show us some of her magic."

"Well, okay," Travis finally said. As they started walking toward the bayou, *Bueno* started following them. "No! You can't go with us," Travis said. He looked at the dog and stomped his foot. "Stay here," Travis kept telling him. The more he tried to make *Bueno* go back home, the more determined he was to follow the boys.

"Oh, let him come," Johnny said.

They hadn't been gone long when they saw an old woman with long stringy black hair, wearing a dirty, ragged red dress.

"Are you the voodoo lady?" Johnny asked.

At his question the old lady smiled, revealing toothless gums. She extended her wrinkled, bony fingered hand toward them.

"Yes. Come with me and I'll show you my magic," she said with an evil chuckle.

She then took a step toward them. Wide-eyed and frozen with fear they stared at her with their mouths open. They took one last look at the woman, looked at each other and bolted with *Bueno* close on their heels. They could hear her wicked cackle as they ran. Out of breath, they finally stopped and looked around.

"Where are we?" Travis asked.

"I–I don't know."

"Are we lost?"

"I think so."

"What are we going to do? Which way should we go? Maybe *Bueno* can show us. Sometimes he's gone all day but he always makes it home by suppertime. He never gets lost.

"Take us home, *Bueno*. Please, show us the way home," Travis said, looking desperately at him.

Bueno turned his head to one side and looked at Travis as he spoke, then turned and trotted off.

"Should we follow him?" Johnny asked.

"Yes. He'll find the way home."

When Charlie Joe came home from visiting a friend, the first thing he asked was, "Where's Travis?"

"He and Johnny are outside," Grace told him.

"No, they aren't," he said. "I looked for them out there before I came inside."

At his words Vivienne and Grace looked at each other in alarm. They jumped up and ran outside, calling the two boys names as loud as they could.

The next door neighbor heard their frantic calls and came out and asked what was wrong.

"We think Travis and Johnny have gone into the bayou," Vivienne said, frantically.

"They asked if they could go see the voodoo woman who supposedly lives out there, and we told them they couldn't. Now we can't find them!" Grace said in desperation.

"I'll saddle my horse and go look for them," he said.

"Oh, thank you!" both mothers said at once.

"Is *Bueno* with them?" Charlie Joe asked.

"I think so. Why?" Vivienne asked.

"Then I have to go with Mr. Pearson."

"You're not going anywhere! You're staying right here!" his mother told him.

"But, if *Bueno's* with them, he'll come to my special whistle."

"Are you sure," his mother asked.

"Yes, ma'am."

"It's worth a try," Grace said, frantically.

As Vivienne and Charlie Joe ran to Mr. Pearson's barn to see if he would let Charlie Joe ride with him, Grace ran home to get her husband.

With only a little persuasion Mr. Pearson lifted Charlie Joe up behind him. By this time Brad Phillips had joined them and they were off in the direction of the bayou.

"Oh, if only Diego were here! He could find them," Vivienne said. She and Grace waited anxiously while the men looked for the boys.

After they got out of sight of the house Charlie Joe let out the loudest and most unusual whistle Mr. Pearson had ever heard. It was met by silence. "Is that your special whistle?" he asked.

"Yes sir." If *Bueno* hears it, he'll come."

"I hope your right."

They rode for about thirty minutes, zig zagging across the area with Charlie Joe whistling every few minutes and Brad Phillips and Mr. Pearson calling to the boys. The sun had just sunk behind the trees when they heard a dog bark.

"That's *Bueno*." Charlie Joe said.

"Are you sure?"

"Yes sir."

With that the men turned their horses in the direction the bark had come from. Suddenly, in the dark shadows, they saw two little boys and a dog running toward them.

After the two lost boys and the dog got on the backs of the horses, behind the two men and Charlie Joe, they headed back to where the anxious mothers awaited them.

When Vivienne and Grace saw them coming toward the house, they ran to meet them. The two women grabbed their sons off the backs of the horses, hugged the boys and shed tears of relief.

After Johnny and his parents had gone home and Vivienne

and the boys and *Bueno* were settled in the parlor Travis said, "We were only lost for a little while. I told *Bueno* to show us the way home and he was doing that when we saw Mr. Phillips and Mr. Pearson. We would have been home in a few minutes."

"Maybe so," Vivienne said, "but you gave us quite a scare. Don't you ever disobey me like that again. Too many bad things could have happened to you out there."

Travis was being brave, but Vivienne could tell he was still scared. After he told her about their encounter with the old woman, she wasn't certain whether it was her or their experience of being lost in the bayou that had scared him the most.

When Diego got home Monday morning the first thing Vivienne told him was about Travis and Johnny's experience in the bayou.

"Did you punish Travis for disobeying you?" he asked.

"No. I thought the fear he experienced seeing that awful woman and the thought of spending the night in the bayou was punishment enough. And I don't think you should punish him either."

"All right. I won't, but I am going to have a long talk with him about why he shouldn't disobey you and scare you like he did. It's not like Travis to do something you've specifically told him he couldn't do."

"I thought we were out of danger's way when we moved to Houston," Vivienne said.

"I'm afraid when little boys are around, danger is always just around the corner. If it doesn't find them, they'll find it," Diego told her.

"He swore *Bueno* would have found the way home," she told him.

"That's probably true, but it most likely wouldn't have happened until supper time or later. I don't think you and Mrs. Phillips could have stood the anxiety of waiting that long," Diego responded.

"If he still wants to see the voodoo woman would you mind if I take him?"

"I guess not," she answered thoughtfully.

A little later, after talking to Travis, Diego said, "I told Travis he should always obey you, no matter how much he doesn't want to, or how convincing his friends may be about doing something you have told him not to.

"When I asked him if he still wanted to go see the voodoo woman he told me in no uncertain terms that he did not.

"Of course Charlie Joe said he wanted to see her. I told him I would take him sometime in the future and if either of them tried to go into the bayou without me they wouldn't be going anywhere for a month.

"In other words you put him off. Are you ever going to take him?" she asked.

"Not if I can help it."

"I'm glad Travis doesn't want to go see her again."

"You're glad! I can't tell you how relieved I was when he told me he didn't want to go."

"I thought you would like to meet a woman with magical powers," Vivienne said.

I have no desire to search the bayou for a voodoo woman with magical powers. I could just imagine her turning me into a snake," he said with a shiver. "I must be getting old."

"They say, 'with age comes wisdom.' It sounds like you might be a little superstitious," Vivienne said, smiling.

"Or a lot superstitious," he admitted.

Chapter 24

Diego was almost asleep when Vivienne shook him awake. "Wake up! Something's wrong. The baby's not due for at least another month, but it's coming now. Go get Doctor Ballard."

Suddenly, Diego was wide awake. He jumped out of bed, and began throwing on his clothes.

"I hate to leave you by yourself but it will only take a few minutes to get the doctor," he said, hoping Dr. Ballard would be home.

"Do you want me to wake Travis? He can go for help if you need it before I get back."

"No. I don't want to scare him. I love you. Please hurry," she said as he bent down and kissed her.

"I'll be back as quick as I can. I love you too," he said. He looked at her and noticed the look of pain and fear on her face.

With those words he was out of the house and running to the stable. After bridling his fastest horse, he jumped on its back without saddling him and raced toward the doctor's house. Within a few minutes he was knocking on Doctor Ballard's door, praying he was there.

When the doctor opened the door, Diego heaved a sigh of relief and told him why he was there and what Vivienne had said.

"You go on home," the doctor told him. "I'll be there as soon as I get dressed and get Mrs. Quinn."

When Diego got back home and went into the bedroom, Vivienne was in labor. He could tell she was already having more pain than she had had when either of the boys were born.

"I love you. Try not to worry. The doctor will be here in a few minutes." He took her hand in his, knelt beside the bed and prayed.

Seth and Maria had only been up a few minutes when there was a loud knock at the front door. When Seth answered it, a Texas Ranger was standing there. Seth's first thought was something had happened to Diego but, when the Ranger handed him an envelope, he noticed the address was in Diego's handwriting.

"I'm sorry to bring you bad news," the Ranger said, quietly, before turning and leaving.

When Seth came into the kitchen and solemnly handed Maria the envelope, she knew immediately something was terribly wrong. Even before opening the envelope she saw it was from Diego and it couldn't have been more than a page long. Diego had never written a short letter.

Maria sat down and opened the letter. With trembling hands she began reading. "This is the hardest letter I have ever had to write," she read. "Monday morning, just after delivering our baby girl, complications set in and Vivienne died."

"No!" Maria cried out.

At those words Seth put his arm around her and held her. Still shaking and holding back her tears, she read the rest of the letter. "I hope you can make it here in time for Vivienne's funeral. It will be Thursday afternoon.

"Our baby girl, Victoria Noelle. is tiny but fine. Mrs. Quinn, Vivienne's mid-wife, is caring for her and the boys until I can make other arrangements.

"Would you please tell Jace and Amber? I don't want them to find out in a letter. Besides, I don't think I could write or say this again. I don't know what I'm going to do without Vivienne. I loved her so much."

After finishing the letter, Maria and Seth looked at each other in disbelief with tears in their eyes.

"I want to go right now to San Antonio and catch the train to Houston. While I pack our things and tell Victoria and Noelle, will you hitch up the buggy?"

"I'll have Antonio tell Miguel and Lila. We'll have one of our *vaqueros* go with us so he can drive us to San Antonio, then bring the buggy back here," Seth offered.

"Our first stop will be to tell Jace and Amber," Maria said a few minutes later as Seth helped her into the buggy.

When they went by Jace and Amber's house on the ranch, Amber wasn't home so they drove into San Pablo to the Marshal's Office.

When they went into the office they were relieved to see Jace and Amber were both there.

"We just received a letter from Diego and I'm afraid he had some very bad news for all of us."

Maria walked over to where Amber was sitting and knelt down in front of her. She looked at her with tears in her eyes, she said, "Vivienne went into early labor. Their daughter is fine but Vivienne didn't survive the complications of the very long labor. I'm so sorry."

"No! NO!" Amber screamed, as she put her hands to her mouth; tears streamed down her face. Jace went to where she was sitting and for several minutes they just held each other.

"What happened?" Jace asked.

"I'm afraid we don't know any of the details. All we know at this time is Vivienne's funeral will be Thursday afternoon. Diego will tell us more when we get to Houston.

"We're on our way now to San Antonio to catch the train to Houston. Will you both be able to go with us?" Maria asked.

"Yes." Amber and Jace said in unison.

After a quick trip to Amber and Jace's house for them to

pack a bag for the trip, they headed to San Antonio and the train station. After a long, tiring and solemn journey they arrived in Houston.

At Seth's knock on the door, Diego opened it. "Mama, Papa, thank you for coming so soon," he said quietly, as he gave his mother a hug.

"We're so sorry about Vivienne," Maria said, as she looked at her son's red eyes and pale, drawn face. *He's still in shock*, she thought to herself.

"How are you holding up?" she asked.

"I don't know," he said quietly.

"Amber and Jace came with us. They said they would feel more comfortable staying at the hotel tonight than they would here. As soon as they get checked in, they'll be here. I know they're anxious to see the children.

"Your father and I thought we might stay here with you to help take care for the children." *And try to help you through this*, she thought. "That is, if it's all right with you."

"Thank you. I would like very much for you to be here. The boys are at school. They stayed home Tuesday and Wednesday but I thought they would be better off going to school today. Mrs. Quinn's in the nursery with Vicky."

"I'm going to go take a peek at her," Maria said. "Hello, Mrs. Quinn. I'm Diego's mother, Maria Black," Maria said when she went into the nursery.

"Hello, Mrs. Black. I'm so sorry about Vivienne."

"Thank you. It's such a shock for all of us. Thank you for stepping in and helping our son and grandchildren during these first few days," Maria replied.

"I'm glad to do it. I wish there was more I could do."

"Oh, you're beautiful," Maria said when Mrs. Quinn handed her the baby. "Except for those big blue eyes, you look like your father did when he was three days old," Maria said as she gave the baby a gentle hug.

"I'm almost sure her eyes are going to stay blue," Mrs.

Quinn said quietly.

"I hope so. With those blue eyes and black hair, she's going to be a real beauty."

"How are the boys doing?" Seth asked.

"A lot better than I am," Diego replied. "It was so unexpected and happened so quickly. You probably understand better than anyone, since your first wife died in childbirth. Do you ever get over the hurt and sense of loss?"

"You'll never completely get over it, but give yourself time. Eventually you'll be able to accept it."

"I hope so. But right now I have my doubts," Diego said quietly.

"Diego, I know you're devastated over losing Vivienne but, remember, you have three children who love you and need you more than ever now. The four of you will help each other get over the loss."

"Seth, I want you to meet our beautiful little granddaughter, Victoria Noelle Black," Maria said when she came into the room carrying their newly born granddaughter.

"She is a beauty," he said. "Are you going to let me hold her?"

"I guess I can let go of her long enough for you to do that," she said.

She smiled as she handed Vicky to him. She looked at Diego and wished with all her heart she could hold him close and kiss the hurt away as she had done when he was a youngster. Sadly, all she could do was to be there and help him pick up the pieces of his shattered life.

"Have you made any plans for what you're going to do?" Maria asked.

"I don't know what I'm going to do. I don't know anything about babies. I don't even know what I'm going to do about the boys. I'm away from home so much of the time," Diego said to his parents, as he looked at Vicky.

"It's too soon for you to know what's best for the children or for yourself. Your father and I talked it over and wondered if you would like for us to keep the children at the ranch until you decide what you're going to do."

"That sounds like a good idea to me but I'll need to talk to the boys and see how they feel about it before I make any final decisions. Thank you for offering."

"It's a long way from Houston to Black Creek. I know you would all miss each other terribly. Think about it as long as you need to. Please don't feel you have to do as I suggested. If you think of another idea, please tell us so we can talk it over together."

Diego then went into the nursery where Mrs. Quinn was and thanked her for all she had done. He told her the children would probably be moving to Black Creek to live and he would no longer be needing her services. Before he could ask, she said she would stay with Vicky that afternoon while the family went to the funeral. He thanked her again, then they went back into the room where his parents were.

While Mrs. Quinn was briefing Maria on Vicky's daily care and routine, Amber and Jace arrived. Maria had been holding Vicky but when Amber came, she handed the baby to her.

Amber sat down in a chair and began feeding Vicky the bottle Maria handed her.

"Can you tell us what happened?" Amber asked, as she looked from Vicky to Diego.

"The baby was turned and the cord was wrapped around her neck. By the time Doctor Ballard managed to deliver Vicky, Vivienne was too weak and had lost too much blood to survive the delivery," Diego explained.

"Did Vivienne get to see Vicky before she…died?" Amber asked.

"Yes. She held her and told her she loved her."

"I'm so thankful for that," Amber said quietly.

"She also got to tell the boys she loved them and for them to help me take care of their little sister.

"Doctor Ballard is one of the best doctors in Houston. He

did all he could to save both of them," Diego said.

"I'm sure he did. Please, don't blame yourself for Vivienne's death. I know you loved her and did all you could for her," Amber assured him.

"The funeral is at four o' clock this afternoon. Mrs. Quinn is going to stay with Vicky while we're gone. I've made arrangements for Vivienne to be taken to Black Creek in the morning so she can be buried in the family cemetery."

While Amber finished giving Vicky her bottle, Maria and Seth left the room so Amber and Jace could have some time alone with Vicky. Seth and Diego went outside and Maria went into the kitchen to make a snack for the boys when they got home from school.

Maria had just taken the cookies out of the oven when she heard the front door open. Going into the front room, she saw Travis and Charlie Joe. When they saw her they stood in silence for a moment, then both came running into her arms and they all hugged.

"Grandma, I'm so glad you came," Travis said.

"I'm glad we're here too," she said.

"Our Mama died," Charlie Joe said, as tears gathered in his eyes.

"I know, sweetheart, and I'm so sorry. I know you both loved your mama very much and you miss her terribly," Maria said as she gave them an extra hug.

"Did Grandpa come too?" Travis asked.

"Yes, he did. And your Grandpa Jace and Grandma Amber are also here."

"Are you going to cook for us?" Travis asked.

"Oh good!" Charlie Joe said when Maria told them she was. "You're a lot better cook than Mrs. Quinn."

"Thank you, dear. Are you hungry?"

"Yes, ma'am!" they both answered.

"I thought you might be. I have a snack for you in the kitchen that you can have as soon as you go into the nursery and greet your Grandma Amber. Your father and grandfathers are outside."

At her words they went to see their grandmother but were soon back for their snack.

"Oh good! Chocolate cookies! We haven't had any of these since…since Mama died," Travis said as a tear made its way down his cheek.

"Well, as soon as I pour you a glass of milk, you can have some."

"How was school today?" Maria asked when they sat down at the table for their snack.

Charlie Joe answered with a simple, "Ugh!" When she asked Travis the same question, his answer was more positive, as she knew it would be.

"We had a test in mathematics today and I didn't miss any of the problems," he said, proudly.

"That's wonderful. I'm very proud of you," his grandmother said. "Is mathematics your favorite subject?"

"Yes, ma'am. That and science."

"Well, Charlie Joe, what's your favorite subject?"

"I don't know," he said with a shrug of his shoulders, as he took another bite of cookie. "I guess reading and recess."

I don't believe recess is considered a school subject, Maria thought with a smile.

"Be sure to save some cookies for Papa," Travis said as Charlie Joe took another one. He likes chocolate cookies too."

"You're right I do like Grandma's chocolate cookies," Diego said as he and Seth and Jace came into the kitchen.

"We've got the buggies hitched up. It's time to go to the funeral."

"We'll be ready as soon as the boys change clothes," she told him.

"Charlie Joe, Travis, I have your change of clothes on your beds," Maria told them. She then ushered them down the hall.

❧

Vivienne and Diego hadn't lived in Houston long but when

the family went into the church for the funeral they were all pleased to see the pews were filled with mourners. The Ranger who had brought the message to Black Creek and another Ranger were standing against the back wall of the church.

After Diego went to the front of the church where the coffin was and said his final good-bye to Vivienne, the rest of the family paid their respects.

Chapter 25

They were up early the next morning to catch the train to San Antonio.

After a small graveside service in the family cemetery, on Black Creek, the family went to the house for supper. Later, when everyone had gone home for the evening, Diego told his parents he had talked to the boys about staying at the ranch for a while. "They both said they want to stay. I told them it would only be until I decide what I'm going to do and see about hiring someone to take care of them and the house."

"Do you also want to stay with us for awhile to help the boys adjust?" Maria asked, thinking the stay at the ranch would also be good for Diego.

"I hadn't considered it but that might be a good idea," he said thoughtfully.

"Son, you know the four of you are welcome to come live on the ranch," Seth told him.

"I've been thinking about that. I would rather the children be reared by the family than a housekeeper. And I know I don't want to be so far away from them. But I'll have to do some serious thinking before I resign from the Rangers."

"You have a lot of plans to make and adjusting to do," Maria said, "but take your time deciding. The decisions you make need to be right ones for all of you."

"This all happened so suddenly. I'm not sure I'm ready to

go back to Houston to an empty house. I think it would probably be best if we did all stay at the ranch for a few days. If you're sure that's all right with you."

"Of course. We will be more than glad to have all of you for as long as you feel you need to stay. Whatever you decide to do will be fine with us," his mother assured him.

"Do you mind if we stay in the big house with you? I would feel rather uncomfortable in our little house without Vivienne being there. I'm sure the boys will feel the same."

"Of course. That's what I had planned on."

The next day, Amber and Jace came for the day.

"Maria," Amber said when the two of them were alone for a few minutes in the kitchen. "You're going to have your hands full keeping up with the boys and Vicky is going to require a lot of time and attention. I hate to separate the children but how would Diego, you and Seth, feel about Jace and me taking Vicky to stay with us?"

"I think it's a very good idea. To be perfectly honest, I'm not sure I can keep up with the boys and give Vicky all the attention she needs. For the next few months she is going to need someone's full, undivided attention. Let's discuss this with Diego to see how he feels about separating the children. Whatever Diego decides will be fine with Seth and me."

I think keeping Vicky will help Amber in her grief of losing Vivienne, Maria thought as she looked closely at her.

At dinner that evening Amber presented her idea to Diego. "Jace and I would like to take Vicky to stay with us. I know she will require a lot of time and attention and I'll have more time than your mother will."

"It's fine with me. How do you feel about it, Mama?"

"That's entirely up to you and the boys. Whatever you decide is fine with your father and me."

"Well. What do the two of you think about that?" he asked Travis and Charlie Joe.

"Do you think it would be all right with Mama?" Travis asked thoughtfully.

Vicky was only five days old but Travis had already formed a big brother, little sister bond with her.

"I think your mother would feel it's just fine. She knows her mother will take good care of Vicky. As far as separating the three of you, it will just be temporary. It will only be until I decide what I'm going to do. I know you'll be able to see your little sister as often as you want."

"Then it's okay with me," Travis said.

"How do you feel about being separated from your little sister?" Diego asked, looking at Charlie Joe.

"It's okay with me. Now we won't have to listen to her crying," Charlie Joe said, turning to his brother.

That brought a smile to everyone's face, thinking it was a typical remark coming from Charlie Joe.

"Thank you all. We'll take her to our house after you leave to go back to Houston," Amber told Diego.

The morning Diego left to return to Houston was a sad one for Travis and Charlie Joe. Maria knew it wouldn't take long for them to again become accustomed to life on the ranch and not being able to see Diego for long periods of time. It was their mother not being there that would be so hard for them to accept.

The boys were adjusting very well to life on the ranch and their new school. Diego came to the ranch to be with them as often as he could. The family all noticed each time he left it was progressively harder on the boys and him.

"I miss *Bueno,*" Travis said sadly, one rainy afternoon when they had spent the day inside and had run out of fun things to do.

"I know you do," Maria said, as she thought desperately for some way to entertain them.

She went to the attic and looked through some trunks.

She found a puzzle and some other toys Diego and his brothers had played with when they were boys. Hopefully, they would help pass the time for Travis and Charlie Joe for a while.

"Like me, Amber is thrilled to have the grandchildren back home. Having Vicky to love and care for is helping her adjust to not having Vivienne. While no one can take the place of a lost child, a grandchild can come closer than anyone. I know it's hard on her when she brings Vicky out here to stay when Diego comes for a visit," Maria said to Seth one evening as they sat on the front porch talking.

"Does she realize that if Diego retires from the Rangers he's going to want Vicky to come live with him?"

"Oh, I'm certain she does."

"Do you think Diego's going to resign from the Rangers?" Seth asked.

"Your guess is as good as mine. But I'm hoping for everyone's sake, he will."

"Noelle is certainly doing a good job with the children. They bring out her maternal instincts. I know she loves them but what surprises me is how firm she can be with the boys."

"Charlie Joe told me she gave him a whipping today," Seth said.

"Yes. And a well deserved one at that. The little rascal was testing her. You should have seen the look of surprise on his face when she turned him over her knee and whipped him. Noelle is extremely good natured, but she doesn't let them take advantage of her. I think she learned not to let anyone take advantage of her when she was married to Darrell.

"Have you noticed Charlie Joe never tries to take advantage of Victoria? I think he knows he wouldn't be able to get away with that."

"Most likely Matthew and Selena have told him how tough their mother can be," Seth told her.

The boys had been at the ranch for a couple of months and Diego was there for one of his rare visits. He had taken the boys to the creek for a couple of hours to fish. When they came back to the house they proudly displayed the string of perch they had caught.

"My goodness, you certainly did well. I know what we'll be having for supper tonight," Maria said.

Both boys beamed at their grandmother's words of praise, and finding out they had provided the evening meal for the family.

"Papa showed us how to scale and gut them," Travis told her, "so they would be ready for you to cook when we brought them home."

"That was fun!" Charlie Joe said.

"That doesn't surprise me. The messier the chore, the more you like it," Maria chuckled.

"I caught more fish than Charlie Joe," Travis said. He looked at his little brother and made a face.

"Well, I caught a turtle. If he hadn't broken the line we could have had turtle soup," Charlie Joe said, making a face back at his brother.

"All right you two, that's enough," Diego said. "After you wash up, go upstairs and put on some clean clothes."

"Do we have to?" they both asked.

Diego didn't say anything, but the look he gave them sent the two little boys scurrying into the washroom.

"That look you just gave the boys was the same one I saw your father give you and your brothers so often when you were youngsters."

"Where do you think I learned it and how well it works?" he asked.

That evening, the family sat on the front porch enjoying the cool evening watching the boys catching fireflies and putting them in a jar.

"Those two are so competitive. Generally Matthew isn't competitive but, when he's around those boys of yours, his competitiveness seems to come out," Victoria said.

"A little competitiveness is good for a person," Diego teased.

"Were Miguel and Antonio and I that competitive when we were that age?" Diego asked his mother.

"Miguel wasn't, but you and Antonio certainly were. I remember one night the two of you got into a fight over which of you had caught the most fireflies."

"What a thing to get into a fight about. But, that does sound like something we would have done," Diego laughed.

"Living in Houston without the children is pure torture for me. I miss so many moments like this," he said thoughtfully as he watched the children. "They change so much between my visits. Especially Vicky. I don't want to be a visitor to them. I want to be their father and to make a home with them.

"I've been doing a lot of thinking and I've decided, if you ladies don't mind being mothers to them on a permanent basis, I'm going to resign from the Rangers and come back out here to live."

"Oh, Diego! We will love having the four of you here permanently. I know the boys will be glad to have you with them all the time," Victoria assured him.

"Have you talked to them about living out here?" Maria asked.

"Yes. They're both thrilled about living on the ranch. I don't know if it's ranch life they like so much or if it's the spoiling their grandmothers and aunts give them."

"I'm proud of you for discussing all your plans with the boys before making any final decisions," Maria said.

"I try to always include them. Their lives are just as affected as mine with every decision I make. Maybe more so. More than anything, I want them to be happy.

"Now I have to find a way to support us. Papa, do you

need another *vaquero*?" he asked with a grin.

It was the first time Maria had seen that devilish, happy grin of his since Vivienne had died. *He'll always love her and miss her, but he's finally beginning to accept life without her,* she thought with a smile of her own.

"Only if he's a good worker and willing to put in twelve hours a day for very little pay," Seth answered, returning the grin.

"Well, I've been away from being a cowboy nearly ten years but you always said I was one of the best *vaqueros* you ever had. So, it shouldn't take me long to remember all I've forgotten."

"I see you haven't lost your sense of humor or your lack of modesty," Seth told him. "It'll be good to have you back, son. Black Creek's missed you."

"We're both glad you have decided to stay. We've all missed you," Maria said. She went over to Diego and gave him a hug. "I think it's the best thing for all of you."

A little later when Maria went inside to check on Vicky, Diego said, "Papa, I'd like to go with you in the morning when you make your rounds of the ranch. I need to talk to you, about some things that are bothering me about my decision."

At breakfast the next morning, when Diego told the boys they were definitely going to move to the ranch they were both thrilled.

"Monday I'm going to Houston to sell the house and pack the rest of our things and have them brought here."

"Are you going to bring, *Bueno*?" Travis asked hopefully.

"Son, I'm going to be coming back on the train. I'm afraid I won't be able to bring him."

All Travis said to his father's remark, as he looked down at his plate was, "Oh."

"Please, Papa. We miss him," Charlie Joe said in the most

pathetic tone Diego had ever heard him use.

It looks like I'm going to have to find some way to make it back with Bueno, he thought as he looked at the sad expressions on his sons' faces. "I'll see what I can do. But I'm not promising anything."

They had been riding for nearly an hour the next morning and Diego hadn't said a word. That alone was an indication to Seth something serious was troubling his son.

"Papa," he finally said, "I thought about asking the Rangers for a transfer to the San Antonio area, but I realized I still wouldn't be able to be with the children anymore than I am now. I know I was away from them more than I was home when Vivienne was alive, but somehow, now that she isn't with them, I feel it's even more important for me to be here for them. Does that make sense?"

Before Seth had a chance to answer the question Diego continued. "I've always felt it was my destiny to be a Ranger and do what I could to help make Texas a better place to live. If I resign from the Rangers, do you think I'll later regret that decision?"

Again, before Seth had a chance to reply Diego continued. "I know Ranger Travis was proud of me for being a deputy Marshal and then following in his footsteps and becoming a Texas Ranger. Do you think he would be disappointed in me if I resign?"

"Son, you're the only person I have ever known who could ask three questions in a row, without pausing to take a breath between questions. If you don't mind, I'll answer your questions one at a time." Seth grinned and then began, "I fully understand why you feel it's so important for you to be a full-time father now. Even though your mother and sisters are filling in quite well as a mother, it's somehow not quite the same. Now, more than ever, they need you.

"I don't think there's a time limit on what it takes to be a good Ranger. Since you joined the force you've been dedicated to the Rangers and have put everything you had into the job. That's all anyone can ask.

"As far as Ranger Travis goes, there's no doubt in my mind he would be proud of the job you have done. I know he would fully understand and agree your family is more important than being a Ranger."

"So, you think the decision I made was the right one."

"You're the only one who can fully answer that question. But, as far as I'm concerned, yes, you made the right decision."

"Thanks, Papa. I knew you would set my mind at ease. Now, let's get back to the job of being ranchers," Diego said with a smile.

CHAPTER 26

As soon as Diego arrived in Houston he went to the house and put a For Sale sign in front of it. He had left both his horses and his saddle at the ranch and come to Houston on the train. So, he hitched up the only horse in the stable and went by buggy to the Texas Ranger office and resigned from the Rangers. When he asked if he could keep his badge, he was told he could. So he put the badge in his pocket and headed back to the house to start packing.

The last thing he did was the hardest of all, packing all of Vivienne's clothes and personal items. He planned to give the two combs her mother had given her as a wedding gift back to Amber. The quilt his mother had given Vivienne as a wedding gift he would give back to her. All her jewelry and some of the other personal items he would give to Amber. Her clothes he would take to the Children's Home in San Pablo. He knew they were always in need of clothing.

That night, as he was getting ready for bed he couldn't bear the thought of sleeping in their bed without Vivienne. So, he made himself as comfortable as he could on the couch. As he was trying to get to sleep, he remembered the only other time he had slept on the couch. That time had eventually had a happy ending. As he thought about that, for the first time since Vivienne had died he broke down. He shed tears for the first time since he was a young boy.

He had been afraid it would take him awhile to sell the house. To his surprise, the second day, as he was filling the last box, a young couple who was moving to Houston came by and agreed to buy the house for the price he was asking.

Since the house on the ranch where they would be moving was already furnished, he had wondered what he was going to do with all their furniture. Fortunately, the couple said they would welcome anything he would leave. After telling them what pieces he would be leaving, he raised the price of the house to include them. The couple gladly accepted the new price. He was now ready to move to Black Creek.

After hitching up the buggy, he took everything he was going to take to Black Creek to the train station and made arrangements for it to be shipped to San Antonio.

While he had been packing, he had tried to figure how to get *Bueno* back to the ranch. He could think of only one way to do that. He didn't like the idea, but it was the only way.

After shipping the furniture he went by the Phillips' house to pick up *Bueno*. While Johnny said his good-byes to *Bueno,* Diego talked with Brad.

"Johnny was hoping you would decide not to come for Bueno. He's turned into a right good dog," Brad told him.

"I'm afraid if I had decided to leave him here I would have had two heart broken sons. I'm not looking forward to the trip back to Black Creek, but, I guess, the looks on Travis and Charlie Joe's faces when they see *Bueno* will be worth the misery I'll go through getting him there. They've lost their mother. The least I can do is let them keep their dog."

That night, after a barely palatable meal around a small campfire, Diego went to the buggy and got his bedroll and put it on the ground. "I can't believe I'm doing this," he said to *Bueno,* as he checked the rope he had tied the dog to the wagon wheel with. "I thought my days of eating my own cooking around a campfire and sleeping on the ground were over.”

With that, he crawled into the bedroll and prepared himself for an uncomfortable night spent on the ground. He was almost asleep when he heard *Bueno* let out a quiet whimper and felt him come over to him and curl up to his side. “I've really gone to the dogs. Or maybe I should say the dogs have come to me.” He laughed as he reached over and petted the dog. Soon they were both asleep.

On the third morning, when Diego rode up to the house tired and hungry, the boys came running out of the house to greet him. Their happy smiles and calm greetings suddenly turned into squeals of happiness when they saw *Bueno.*

“You brought him,” Travis exclaimed excitedly. He lifted the dog from the seat of the buggy and gave him a hug.

“He's almost as excited to see you as you are to see him,” Diego said, as he saw *Bueno's* trail wagging furiously with happiness as he licked Travis' face. “I advise you to put him down for a minute before you regret it.”

Sure enough, as soon as the dog's feet touched the ground, he ran to one of the buggy wheels and raised his leg. Before the boys could catch him he had made a circle around the buggy, raising his leg to each of the wheels.

“I'm glad to see you found a way to get him here,” Maria said, as she came out of the house. “You have again become a hero in your sons' eyes.”

“I better warn you now,” Diego said, as they watched the boys and the dog chasing each other around the yard, “as hard as Vivienne tried, she never managed to get *Bueno's* bed out of the kitchen and into the yard.”

“I can deal with that. If you will recall, I had that same problem with you and your brothers and the three of you won.

“Although it's mid-morning, I'm almost certain you didn't fix yourself breakfast this morning, she said.

The look on his face told her she was right. “After you put the horse and buggy up, come in the kitchen and I'll fix you something to eat.”

“I'm as excited about a good meal as they boys are about

having *Bueno*. Give me ten minutes and I'll be ready for a plate full of your good hot cakes and maybe some bacon and eggs, and whatever else you want to fix." He grinned with satisfaction.

"Diego," Maria told him later that evening, "supper's almost ready. Will you find the boys and have them wash up?"

"It's time to go clean up for supper," he said when he went out on the porch and saw Charlie Joe playing by himself. "Do you happen to know where your brother is?"

"I think he's in the barn."

"What's he doing there?" Diego asked.

"I don't know," Charlie Joe said, quietly. He shrugged his shoulders as he went into the house.

When Diego got to the barn he could hear Travis quietly talking but he didn't hear anyone else. He went around to the back of the barn and saw his son sitting on the ground holding *Bueno*. The dog was licking tears off Travis' cheeks.

Diego stepped around to the side of the barn and out of Travis' sight. He heard his son say, "I miss Mama so much. Why did God have to take her back to Heaven?

"Sometimes I don't like Vicky. If she hadn't been born, I'd still have Mama," he said bitterly.

How can I explain to him Vicky's not to blame for his mother's death? Diego thought. *It looks like I'm going to have to talk to Mama about this. I know she'll be able to tell me how to explain the situation to Travis so he'll understand.*

After listening a little longer, Diego, not wanting to embarrass his son by letting him know he had seen him crying, stepped inside the barn and called out, "Travis! Travis, where are you? Supper's ready."

"I'll be there in a minute," he heard his son say.

"Don't be long. You know your grandmother doesn't like it when someone's late for a meal." With that he went back to the house, giving Travis time to dry his tears before he came to the house.

After supper when the boys had gone to their rooms and it was just Diego and his parents in the library, he decided now was as good a time as any to talk to his mother about overhearing Travis talking to *Bueno*.

"You're not able to be around the children enough to notice how differently the boys respond to Vicky. Charlie Joe is always happy to play with her. Although Travis is very protective of her when she wants him to play with her, he nearly always finds something else to do," she said after he told her about what he had overheard. "I knew it was out of character for Travis, but I didn't know the reason for his strange behavior. I thought he was probably a little jealous of her, but now I know it goes deeper than that."

"What should I do or say to him to let him know Vicky isn't responsible for his mother's death?" he asked. "I don't want him growing up having resentment toward his sister over something she had no control over."

"That's a hard question to answer," she said thoughtfully. "You'll need to talk to him and listen carefully to everything he says. Try to answer his unasked questions, as well as the ones he asks. Would you like for me to talk to him?" she asked when she saw the look of confusion on his face.

"I hate to push another problem off on you, but I'm afraid I'm not any good at reading the childrens' thoughts. I have a hard enough time answering their easy questions."

"I'll be glad to talk to him about it."

"Thank you. I know you'll be able to explain the situation to him better than I would be able to."

"He will probably still have some questions only you can answer. Even if he doesn't, you still need to talk to him about his mother. I know it will be hard on you but you need to keep Vivienne a part of both the boys lives as much as possible."

"I know and I do want to do that."

CHAPTER 27

Maria was looking out the window when she saw Cody ride up to the house with Seth, sitting limply on the saddle in front of him. Cody had one arm around Seth to help steady him and Maria saw blood on his shirt.

"What happened?" she cried in alarm, as she came running out of the house.

"He's been shot!" Cody said. He lifted Seth from the saddle.

"Let's take him into the parlor and put him on the daybed," she instructed. She put her arm around Seth and helped Cody carry his limp body up the steps and into the house.

When they had him settled, she saw his breathing was very weak and by the way the fibers on his shirt were laying, she could tell the bullet had come out near his heart. "Go find the rest of the family and have them come here, fast."

"I'll get the doctor."

"I'm afraid that won't be necessary," she said quietly.

After looking at her in surprise, Cody left the room.

She took Seth's hand in hers, knelt beside him, crossed herself and prayed. Noelle must have heard the commotion because she came running down the stairs and into the room. Without a word she knelt beside her mother.

Just as Seth slowly opened his eyes and looked at Maria, Victoria came rushing into the room. "Oh, Papa!" she said quietly. With tears in her eyes, she knelt beside her mother and sister.

"I love you. What happened?" Maria asked softly.

"Darrell. Ambush," he said weakly.

At her father's words, a quiet gasp was heard from Noelle.

A weak smile crossed his face. "I love you." With those whispered words he gave Maria's hand a gentle squeeze, then closed his eyes for the final time.

Maria put her head on his shoulder and knelt there shedding silent tears for several minutes.

She looked up, with tears streaming down her face and saw Antonio, Cody and Diego had joined the others. "Has someone gone for Miguel and Lila?" she asked.

"They're on their way," Cody answered quietly.

"We'll leave now so you can have some time alone with Papa," Victoria told her.

"Thank you."

When Maria went into the library later, she was relieved to see Miguel and Lila had joined the rest of the family.

"What happened?" Miguel asked.

"All he said was Darrell ambushed him," Maria told him.

"That damned son-of-a-bitch. I'm going to kill the cowardly, no-good, back-shooting bastard!" Diego said angrily, through clinched teeth.

"I think we all wish him dead. Please, don't do anything illegal," his mother pleaded.

"I won't. But, I promise you, he'll pay for this!"

"I thought he was still in prison," Antonio said. "When did he escape?"

"I'm going into town and send a telegraph to Huntsville and find out what happened. Then I'm going to contact every Texas Ranger I know. I promise we'll have Darrell in our hands before the end of the week," Diego said. With those words he left the house and headed for San Pablo and the telegraph office.

"Oh, this is all my fault," Noelle sobbed. "If I hadn't

married Darrell and divorced him, this never would have happened."

"It's not your fault, Noelle," Maria assured her. "It was just your father's time to go. He was much happier dying the way he did, rather than from a lengthy, painful illness. He was in very little pain and it was relatively quick. Please, don't blame yourself."

"Mama, I'll go into San Pablo and make the funeral arrangements. Do you have any special requests?" Miguel asked.

"Thank you. Your father always said he wanted a small, simple funeral. We can't control how many people will be there but, please, be sure it's not elaborate."

When Travis and Charlie Joe came in from school a little later even they could feel something was the matter. The first thing Travis said was, "What's wrong?"

Noelle looked at Maria and then told the boys to sit down, that she had some very sad news for them. "I'm afraid your Grandpa Seth has been killed."

After a moment of stunned silence Charlie Joe asked what had happened.

"He was shot," Noelle told him.

"Who shot him?" he asked.

Noelle took a deep breath before answering in a shaking voice, "Darrell."

Neither of the boys said anything as they went over to their grandmother. Maria put her arms around them and drew them close while they cried.

"We have to be strong," Maria told them, as they pulled away and looked at her.

"I'm going to miss him," Charlie Joe told her.

"I know. I'm going to miss him too," Maria said.

Looking at Charlie Joe, Maria saw shock and grief but there was also something else there. *Was it anger?* she wondered.

"Why is everybody I love dying?" Travis asked.

"I don't know sweetheart," Maria said, wondering the same thing herself.

When Miguel returned later that afternoon, he told them the arrangements had been made. The funeral would be the next afternoon at three o'clock.

"I saw Diego while I was in town. He got word from Huntsville that Darrell escaped from prison night before last. A Ranger Diego contacted in Houston will be here tomorrow. He also said Captain Jones was catching the next train out of San Angelo and will also be here sometime tomorrow. When they get here, they'll meet up in Jace's office.

"In the meantime, Cody is showing Diego where he found Papa. Diego's going to see if he can find where Darrell was headed after the shooting. Since Darrell has nowhere to go, he's not going to have any choice but to live off the land until he can make it to somewhere he isn't known. Diego promised he would be back here in time for the funeral."

"Mama, I just went to the bunkhouse to let the *vaqueros* know when the funeral was going to be. Several of them would like to come now to pay their respects if it's all right with you," Antonio told her a few minutes later.

"Of course. I would appreciate that very much."

After Diego found where Darrell had ambushed his father, he followed the trail until the fading light made it too dark to see the tracks. He considered returning to the ranch for the night but decided to camp where he was so he could start tracking again at first light. He would have time to track for several hours in the morning, before going back for the funeral.

He tied his horse to a tree, took the saddle off and put it on the ground. Using the saddle for a pillow, he settled down for the night.

At daybreak he was up and on the trail again. Shortly after noon, having made good headway, he headed back to the ranch. Cleaning up a bit, he went to the big house and joined the rest of the family who had all gathered to go to the church for the funeral.

After tying his horse to the back of Victoria and Cody's buggy, he got into the buggy with them.

"Did you have any luck picking up Darrell's trail?" Victoria asked when he got into the buggy.

"Yes."

"Good. We all had faith that you would. Cody and I made a pack for you, with a bedroll and some food and other things you'll need to continue on the trail."

"Thanks. I'm leaving right after the funeral. I just hope it doesn't rain or the wind doesn't wipe out the tracks before we find him.

"Have you had word if Captain Jones or anyone else has made it to San Pablo?" he asked Cody.

"Captain Jones is there but no one else has made it."

"As long as Captain Jones made it, that's all that matters. The two of us can take care of Darrell."

When the family went into the church, no one was surprised to see the pews were filled and people were lined up along the walls.

I haven't seen the church this full for a funeral since my father died, Maria thought as she walked to the front of the church where the coffin was.

The coffin was closed but that didn't prevent her from feeling his presence. After crossing herself, she knelt and said a short silent prayer. Then standing, she put her hands on the top of the coffin and said quietly, "Seth, I told Miguel to make the funeral simple and it appears he did, but we had no control over how many people would be here. I forgot to ask Miguel to tell Father Michael to make the ceremony short, but I think the good Father knew you and your impatience well enough to do that without being told.

"I love you. You will always be with me in my heart." With those words she crossed herself again, walked to the pew and sat down while the rest of the family went to the casket to pay their respects.

"I'm going with you," Antonio told Diego after the service, as he was preparing to continue his search for Darrell.

"No, you aren't," Diego said firmly.

"Yes, I am! He was my father too!"

"The Captain, Lieutenant Mitchell and I will be able to take care of Darrell. I don't want to have to worry about you and I certainly don't want Mama worrying about you."

"What about you? She's going to worry about you."

"She's use to worrying about me. Don't argue with me about this. I can out argue you and I can still beat the hell out of you and I'll do just that if you try to go with us. Besides, you need to stay here and help guard Noelle."

"All right," Antonio said reluctantly.

Diego then went to his mother and told her they were leaving to find Darrell and wouldn't be back until they did. "I hope you don't mind, but I'm not going to the graveside service. I don't want Darrell to get any farther ahead of us than he already is."

"I understand. Please, be careful," she said.

"I'll do my best," he said as he gave her a hug.

With that he went to where Captain Jones and Lieutenant Mitchell were waiting. "Thank you both for coming."

"Diego, I'm really sorry about your father. I regret I never had the opportunity to meet him. I know he was an exceptional man," Captain Jones, said.

"Thank you, sir."

"How is your mother doing?"

"As well as can be expected. She loved Papa very much and is going to miss him terribly, but she's a strong woman."

"Elizabeth and I were very saddened when we got your letter about Vivienne. We both cared a lot for her. She was a very special lady. I know these past months have been very hard on you and the boys."

"Thank you and Elizabeth for your kind thoughts."

"Diego," Jace said, as he came up to him, "I'm prepared to go with you if you would like me to."

"Thanks for the offer. I appreciate it but I think Captain Jones, Lieutenant Mitchell and I can take care of Darrell. It would mean a lot to me and the family if you would stay here and help Antonio watch out for Noelle. I think Darrell's out for her also. In fact, I don't think anyone in the family is safe until that damn bastard is dead."

"All right. If you're sure you don't need me, I'll stay here." With Diego's confirmation, Jace walked over to where Amber and the rest of the family stood.

After talking to a few more people who had come to pay their respects, the three men headed to where Diego had left Darrell's trail to come back for the funeral. As they rode, Diego told the two Rangers what had happened.

"He didn't go to any trouble to cover his tracks," Lieutenant Mitchell said, as he looked at the tracks.

"He probably didn't know Papa had seen him or lived long enough to tell anyone who had shot him. Have you noticed the trail is going due south? I'm almost certain he's headed for Mexico."

"Diego, I know it's been a while since you resigned from the Rangers but did you happen to bring your Ranger badge with you?" Captain Jones asked.

"Yes sir. As a matter of fact I did."

"I think it might be a good idea if you put it on. We'll get more respect from anyone we talk to if they think we're all Rangers."

"I was hoping you would say that," Diego said. He took the badge out of his pocket and pinned it to his shirt.

"However, we'll all have to remove our badges and go as average citizens if he should make it across the border. The Rangers don't have any authority in Mexico."

"You don't mind doing that?" Lieutenant Mitchell asked in surprise.

"Not in the least. You'd be surprised how many men are caught on the other side of the Rio Grande and brought back across the river to stand trial."

"I might as well tell you now, I have no intention of Darrell going to trial," Diego stated bitterly.

The captain didn't say anything.

"If we should see anyone to question, let me do the talking," the captain said a few minutes later.

"Diego, I know you don't want to stop tracking, but, I think it best we call it quits for the day. We don't want to lose the trail due to the fading light," the captain said a little later.

Diego reluctantly agreed and they made camp for the night.

They had only been on the trail a short while the next morning when Captain Jones said, "Have you noticed the tracks are gradually veering west?"

Diego had been so intent on following the tracks he had failed to notice. "Damn! The son-of-a-bitch is doubling back to Black Creek."

"Are you sure?" Lieutenant Mitchell asked.

"Yes! He's after Noelle," Diego exclaimed. He dropped the lead rope of the pack horse. He turned his horse and spurred him toward the ranch.

After Lieutenant Mitchell picked up the rope of the pack horse, he and the captain followed Diego. As they raced toward the ranch, Diego pulled ahead of the others. He was still nearly a mile from the house when he heard a gunshot. He leaned low over his horse's neck, and drew his rifle from the saddle holster and cocked it.

As he cleared the last strand of trees he saw a horseman riding down the hill toward him. He could tell, without a doubt, it was Darrell. Silently, he aimed his rifle and fired.

The last he saw of Darrell the man had fallen from the saddle. One foot was hooked in the stirrup and his horse was dragging him through the trees.

As Diego reined his horse to a stop he saw Antonio carrying Noelle into the house.

"She's been shot," he told Diego, "in the back."

"Antonio, would you go for Doctor Brown? That bullet is going to have to come out as soon as possible," Maria told him as he lay Noelle down on the daybed.

"Are you in much pain?" Maria asked.

"No."

That's strange, Maria thought. *Considering where the bullet entered and the fact it's still in, I would think she would be feeling a great deal of pain.*

Suddenly an alarmed look crossed Noelle's face and she shrieked, "Mama, I can't move my legs!"

The family all looked at each other in shock, too stunned to say anything.

"Don't try to move. Doctor Brown will be here in a few minutes," Maria told her.

Diego took Antonio firmly by the arm and lead him out of the room. He then demanded to know why Noelle had been outside.

"She went to ask Victoria something. None of us knew she had left the house. I came around the corner of the house just as she got hit. Darrel was hiding behind that dense strand of trees behind the house," Antonio told him.

"I heard a gunshot just before I saw you. Was it you firing?" Antonio asked.

"Yes. We don't have to worry about Darrell anymore. He's dead."

"Good," Antonio said.

The doctor arrived shortly. After examining Noelle he said solemnly, "The bullet shattered several discs in your back. I'm afraid you've lost the use of your legs."

While the rest of the family gasped in horror and shock, Noelle quietly said, "This is my punishment for being the reason Papa was killed."

"Oh, Noelle. Please don't feel that way," Maria said. She forced a faint smile to her lips, hoping to console her daughter.

"Don't worry, Mama. I can handle this. With all of your help, of course. What about Darrell?" she asked looking at Diego.

"He's dead," Diego told her.

"Good," she answered. A smile, a look of relief and satisfaction crossed her face.

"Noelle, I'm going to have to remove the bullet. I'll give you something to help ease the pain but I'm afraid it's still going to hurt," Doctor Brown told her.

"What can we do to help?" Maria asked.

"I'll need some boiled water to sterilize my instruments and some strips of cotton cloth to make bandages."

"I'll take care of that," Victoria told him. With that she left the room, followed by everyone except Maria.

Diego went outside and saw the captain and lieutenant standing beside their horses.

"How's your sister?" the captain asked.

"The bullet shattered several discs in her back. The doctor said she's lost the use of her legs."

"I'm very sorry to hear that. Is she in much pain?" Lieutenant Mitchell asked.

"She says she's in very little pain."

"How's she taking the news that she won't be able to walk?" Captain Jones asked.

"You'd have to know my sister to understand that she said she could handle it with everyone's help," Diego told him.

"Considering she's your sister, that really doesn't surprise me. You've got a very strong and supportive family."

"Yes, I do. I want to thank you both for all the help you've given me the past couple of days."

"I'm sorry, we couldn't have stopped him before he shot your sister," Lieutenant Mitchell said.

"I am too, but we all did the best we could. If you'll take Darrell's body into San Pablo to the morgue, I would appreciate it."

"We'll be glad to," Captain Jones said. "The rifle he used was the most high-powered and expensive gun I've ever seen, outside a gun shop."

"And without a doubt, stolen," Diego added.

"I have no problem with the fact I killed him but is the law going to question my decision?"

"Don't worry about that. After all, he was an escaped convict and murderer. If the law does question his death they'll have me to answer to," Captain Jones reassured him.

"Thanks. Here's the information you'll need about Darrell for the undertaker. If he has any questions, he knows where to find me.

"On behalf of the family, I thank you both for all the help you've been," Diego said. after they had put Darrell across his saddle. The two Rangers rode off to complete the assignment.

CHAPTER 28

"Mama," Noelle said several days later, "I've been thinking about what I'm going to do after I'm able to get around. I would like to continue teaching. but getting to the school and back everyday would be a lot of trouble for everyone, myself included.

"How do you feel about me working in the Children's Home in San Pablo instead? I know it's farther from here than the school, but I could have a room there so that I could stay several days at a time. When the weather's bad, I won't have to worry about going back and forth."

"That sounds like a wonderful idea if you're sure that's what you want to do. I know Mr. and Mrs. Harper will be thrilled to have your help.

"The only person who won't be happy about your decision will be Mr. Jamison. He's going to miss having you at the school."

"I'm going to miss teaching, but I'm sure I want to work in the Children's Home. The only thing is I won't be making any money to support myself."

"Don't you worry about that for a minute. The encouragement and love you will be giving the children will be worth more than anything money can buy."

"Do you think the rest of the family will feel the same way?"

"Oh, sweetheart, I know they will."

"Marcus and I talked about it when he was here today and

he also thinks it's a good idea."

"He's been coming to see you a lot lately," Maria said, hoping she would learn something more about their relationship.

All Noelle said to her mother's remark was, "Yes, he has."

Work began on the Children's Home, as well as the main house, to accommodate a wheelchair.

One chilly February morning, as Maria was hanging clothes on the line to dry, she kept hearing a dull thump-- thump noise coming from the direction of the barn. When she finished her chore she went to investigate the sound.

She went around the corner of the old barn, and saw Charlie Joe throwing rocks at a figure of a man he had drawn on the wall of the barn with chalk. She watched him for a few minutes, and seeing the look on his face she knew, without a doubt, who the figure represented.

"What are you doing?" she asked.

Without taking his eyes from the figure he threw another rock and said, "I'm pretending that's Darrell and these are big rocks I'm throwing at him."

"Please stop for a few minutes and let's talk about this," she said. She walked over to where he was standing and put her arm around him. "Why are you doing that?"

"Everyone I love is dying and I don't know why. I sort of understand why Mama died and God left Vicky in her place. But, I don't understand why Grandpa died. I miss them so much." As he talked the tears that had been brimming in his eyes began rolling down his cheeks.

"I don't fully understand myself. Let's go sit on that bench under the tree and talk about it.

"We all thought Darrell was a nice person. Not long after he and your Aunt Noelle married she began seeing what a bad person he was. She left him and came home. That made him very angry. It was after that your Grandpa started looking to see if there were other bad things about Darrell and found more than he bargained for. It seems Darrell and some other men, his own father included, were stealing money from other people and they had tried to kill the governor. When that was discovered, Darrell and his father were sent to prison.

"Darrell was very angry at your grandpa and Aunt Noelle because he didn't think what he and his father had tried to do was bad. He felt it was all Grandpa and Aunt Noelle's fault he was in prison. So, while he was there he started planning to kill them. He was a wicked person who thought he could do no wrong."

"I hate him," Charlie Joe said bitterly.

"Hate is such an ugly feeling. God doesn't like for us to feel that way about another person no matter how bad they may be. Remember, Darrell is dead and the only person you are hurting by feeling that way is yourself."

"Is he going to Hell?" Charlie Joe asked.

"I don't know. That decision is one only God can make. We must leave his final punishment to God."

"Am I suppose to forgive him for what he did?"

"I know it's hard, but try."

"Have you forgiven him?"

"I'm working on it and I would like for you to do the same. Will you try?"

"I'll try. But it won't be easy," he said after a moment of thought.

"That's all I ask. Now, let's forget about Darrell and go make some hot chocolate. It's getting chilly out here," Maria said. She smiled and ruffled his hair.

After supper that night, when the boys had gone into the other room to play and Noelle had gone to her room, Maria told Diego about the conversation she had had with Charlie Joe that morning.

"I hope I didn't say too much. After all, he is only ten years old."

"What you said was fine. I remember hearing you tell Papa, 'If a child is old enough to ask a question, he's old enough to get an honest answer.' You answered his question better and a lot more diplomatically than I would have been able to. Thank you for taking care of the situation. I'm sorry you had to go through that."

"That's all right. It was a reminder to me that I too should forgive."

"Mama, I'm going into San Antonio tomorrow to get some supplies for the ranch," Miguel told Maria a few days later. "Would you like for me to find a wheelchair for Noelle while I'm there? I'm going to take the wagon, so I'll have plenty of room."

"Yes. That would be good. She's about ready to start getting around."

"I know you have your hands full, but Lila said she would like to go with me if you could keep Daniel while we're gone. If it's not too much trouble."

"It won't be any trouble. If you can bring him a change of clothes by this afternoon, he can come home from school with his cousins today and have an extra day with them. When you leave here you can go by the school and let Mr. Jamison know to let Daniel come home with them."

"Are you sure?" Miguel asked.

"Yes. Now go and tell Lila so she can do what she needs to do before you leave."

"Thanks. You are a saint."

"So I've been told," Maria said with a laugh.

Noelle had only had her wheelchair a few days when she announced she was ready to start working at the Children's Home. The next morning, Antonio and Diego drove her there and got her settled.

To everyone's surprise, when she returned home that evening, she told the family she wanted to go back the next day and stay for several days. Maria was concerned that it would be too much for her to handle so soon after being up and learning to use the wheelchair. After questioning her in detail, Maria was finally convinced she would be able to handle the stay.

For the past month Noelle had been spending more time at the Children's Home than she was spending at home. It didn't seem to be as hard on her as they had feared it would be. It was apparent she was happier than she had been in a long time. Maria wondered if the attention Marcus was paying her might also be part of the reason she was so happy.

Maria had gone outside to sweep the leaves off the porch and was thinking about Noelle when Marcus rode up.

"It's good to see you, Marcus," Maria said as he was getting off his horse. "I'm afraid Noelle isn't here. She's at the Children's Home."

"Yes ma'am, I know. I just came from there. I'm here to talk to you. I wanted you to be the first in your family to know I asked Noelle again to marry me and this time she said yes," he said with a big smile.

"Oh, Marcus. I'm so happy for both of you!"

"Thank you."

"I was afraid you had given up on her ever accepting your proposal."

"I love her too much to have ever done that. I would have kept asking until she said yes, no matter how long it took.

"I want you to know I have no reservations about marrying her because she's confined to a wheelchair. She's still the sweet, beautiful person she's always been.

"My parents are thrilled about us getting married. They're going to build us a house next to theirs that will have ramps and wide doors to comfortably accommodate a wheelchair. And, the wife of one of our cowboys, who Noelle has met and likes very much, has offered to help her with the cooking and other household duties.

"I haven't talked to Miguel but I'm hoping he will draw the plans for the house."

"Oh, I'm sure he'll be happy to," Maria told him. "It sounds you've put a lot of thought into this."

"Yes ma'am, I have. Although she didn't give me a final yes until today, I've known for several days she was finally going to accept my proposal. I hope you don't mind her moving from here."

"Not at all. Of course I'll miss her, but I know she'll be happy married to you and living on the Running W. Since you're going to be married to my daughter, you can start calling me Maria, instead of Mrs. Black," she said with a smile.

"Thank you. That's going to be rather hard to do, since I've called you Mrs. Black all my life. Do you think Mr. Black would have approved of Noelle marrying me?"

"Oh, yes! Seth and I had both hoped the two of you would marry when you first started showing a romantic interest in each other, when you were both just youngsters."

"In spite of all the mischief Diego and I got into when we were kids?"

"Actually, because of that. Noelle has always been rather reserved and Seth and I both felt your mischievous personality would be good for her. You have both our blessings."

"Thank you. I'm going to go get Noelle now. When we get back we'll make our announcement. Would it be possible to have everyone here when we make our announcement?

"Oh, one more thing. Would you please act surprised when we tell the family. I don't want Noelle to know I came to talk to you beforehand. And please don't say anything to the rest of the family. I want everyone to be truly surprised."

"It will be hard, but I promise to keep your secret. Please, plan on staying for supper tonight. I know we will all have a lot of questions for the two of you."

"Thank you, ma'am. I'll be glad to do that," Marcus said and smiled again.

She wanted all the family to be present when Noelle and Marcus made their announcement. The only way she knew to have everyone there, without telling them about the engagement beforehand, was to have everyone for supper. *That's a lot of people to have for a meal and I don't have much time. The first thing I'll need to do is to ask Carlotta if she can help me. I'd better get busy*, she thought.

After sending one of the men to Miguel's house to invite him and his family for supper, she began asking the other children and their families.

Fortunately, she was so busy for the next couple of hours she didn't have time to worry about keeping the secret.

When the family, all sixteen of them, had gathered in the library before supper, Marcus stood beside Noelle's chair and said in a tone loud enough to be heard over the noise of everyone talking, "May I have your attention!" When the room was quiet he said, "As you all know, I've been asking Noelle for her hand in marriage for a long time now. I'm happy and proud to tell you that today she finally accepted."

After Noelle and Marcus had been congratulated by all the family, Maria asked if they had set a date for the wedding.

"Not yet," Marcus said looking at Noelle. "But, since your and Mr. Black's thirty-fifth wedding anniversary is coming up in April, we thought we would like to be married on that date. That is, if it's all right with you."

"Oh, how sweet! Seth and I would both be honored for you to marry on that date," Maria said. She got up and went over to Noelle and gave her a big hug.

"That doesn't give you much time to make plans for a wedding," Victoria said.

"It's time enough. I've waited too long already to make this beautiful lady my wife. I don't want to wait any longer."

"Actually, we talked about it and we both want a small wedding. So it shouldn't take much planning," Noelle said. She looked at Marcus and smiled.

"Marcus and I have some more news for you," Noelle told them. "We have decided, after we've been married for a while and settled in the house, we're going to adopt a couple of children from the Children's Home."

There was a stunned silence for a moment before Maria

asked, "Are you sure that won't be too hard on you?"

"No. Marcus and I have talked this over and have decided we really want to do it. Neither of us feel it will cause any sort of hardship on either of us."

"Do you know which children you want to adopt?" Victoria asked.

"Yes. Chloe and Christopher. A girl for me and a boy for Marcus," Noelle said with a big smile.

"Oh goodie!" Selena exclaimed. "A girl for me to play with!"

"They're both good children and old enough they won't be a physical burden on Noelle," Marcus told them.

"You chose well. I think they will both be a joy to you," Maria said.

Suddenly the room was again filled with congratulations and laughter. Plans for the wedding were soon underway.

When Diego went into the barn a few afternoons later he saw his mother in the stall with his father's horse. She had her head resting on his neck and was gently rubbing his shoulder.

As he unsaddled his horse and was brushing him, Diego watched his mother. After he put a bucket of feed in the horse's trough, he walked over to her.

"Is something wrong?" he asked.

"No," she answered quietly.

He opened the stall door, and went to her. He gently turned her toward him and saw the tears in her eyes.

"You're thinking about Papa, aren't you? You still miss him terribly, don't you?"

"Yes. The pain of missing him doesn't seem to be easing up in the least."

"Give yourself a little more time."

"Is that a bit of fatherly advice coming from you, my son?"

"I guess it is," Diego said thoughtfully. "After all, I too have lost someone I loved dearly and I am a father."

"Please, don't say anything to Noelle about what I just said. She still feels guilty about your father's death."

"Don't worry. Your secret is safe with me." With that, he put his arm around her shoulders and they walked to the house.

CHAPTER 29

"What brings you back to the house in the middle of the afternoon?" Maria asked when Diego came into the kitchen where she had just taken a cake out of the oven.

"I was in San Pablo and smelled this cake baking." He grinned, and picked up a knife and cut himself a piece.

"Young man, if you were just a little younger, I'd turn you over my knee and whip you for that."

"There are advantages to being over thirty and bigger than you," he said. He winked and took a bite of the cake. "Mmm, this is delicious."

"Thank you. Now do you want to tell me the real reason you're here?"

"You're still corresponding with Papa's brother's wife, Aunt Anna, aren't you?" he asked.

"Yes."

"Would you write and ask her if we could buy a couple of their horses?

"I want to get some more of that good Arabian blood into our horses. I know the family there is still financially strapped since the war. So, be sure to tell them I'll pay top price for the horses and will pay to have them transported here. I know the train goes through Richmond and that's not far from where they live."

"I'll write Anna and ask her. I'm sure they'll be happy to sell you as many horses as you want. School will be out for the summer in another month. Why don't you and the boys go to Willoughby and get the horses? I know they'll love the train ride and it will be a wonderful experience for them. That way you can personally pick out the horses you want."

"That's a good idea! Do you trust me to take good care of your grandsons, without your supervision, for the length of time we'll be gone?"

"If you're not good to them, I can count on Charlie Joe reporting back to me with that information."

"That's not reporting. That's what you call tattling," he laughed.

"Either way, it will keep you in line."

"Do you want to go with us?"

"No, thank you. Even on the train that's too long a trip for my liking. I'll stay here and help take care of Vicky."

"Thank you. The boys will be thrilled to find out they'll have the time away from their little sister. I know they both love her, but she's getting to the age now where she seems to enjoy annoying them. She reminds me more of Victoria every day and how she use to pester Miguel and Antonio and me.

"Now, I'd better get back to being a cowboy. I need to earn my keep and the money to buy those horses." He cut another piece of cake and walked out the door.

The week after school was out Antonio drove Diego and the boys to San Antonio to the train station. They were on their way to Virginia.

The first two days the boys were so excited about the train ride they were happy and in a good mood. But, by the third day they were getting restless and Diego was wishing his mother had come with them.

"Welcome home," Maria said when she went into the barn and saw Diego putting feed into one of the horse's stall.

"Thanks. It's good to be home. I'd give you a hug but I'm afraid I'm all dirty," Diego said looking down at his clothes.

"Some children never outgrow wearing their good clothes to do dirty work in," she said. She looked at his ruined traveling suit and shook her head.

"Sorry, but I had to get these horses put up before I did anything else.

"Where are the boys?" Diego asked.

"After a quick hello to me they ran off to tell Matthew about their adventures in Virginia."

"I'm sure they're going to embellish greatly on them when they tell Matthew."

"I'm sure they will. They are their father's sons," Maria remarked.

"Did they change clothes before they took off?" he asked.

"Yes. I have a little more control over them than I do their father. I not only count twice as many horses as you said you were going to bring back, but your sons told me you also brought back a cousin."

"Oh, sorry. I almost forgot to introduce you. Robert, where are you?" Diego called out. At his words a tall, slender, young man came out of the tack room.

"Right here," he answered.

"Mama, meet Robert Lee Black, Uncle James and Aunt Anna's son and my cousin. Robert, this is my mother, your aunt, Maria Black."

"Very pleased to meet you, ma'am," Robert said as he bowed to her.

"Oh, those wonderful southern manners! I'm afraid you'll find your Texas relatives don't have your eloquent style," Maria said. She looked at Diego and smiled.

"Now let's go to the house so you can meet the rest of the family. Since Diego didn't tell us you were coming, I'm afraid we didn't prepare for you. Are you here for a visit or are you going to stay?"

"I said so many good things about Texas and all of the family here, Robert decided he wanted to come here and live."

"I'd like to hear what Robert has to say. I'm sure he can answer my questions even better than you can," Maria said, gently reprimanding Diego.

"Sorry. I do, sometimes, have a tendency to express my opinion when it's not needed or wanted," Diego said.

"That is an understatement," his mother said with a smile.

"Robert, you look so much like your father. You have his blond hair and soft blue eyes," Maria said.

"Thank you, ma'am."

Before they reached the house Victoria came out carrying Vicky.

When she put Vicky down the little girl came running to Diego with outstretched arms, "Papa," she said. He leaned down and swooped her into his arms.

"You remember me!" he said proudly.

"Fi, Fi," she said.

At that he held her up above his head and whirled her around while she laughed and said, "Mo, mo."

"That's all for now, little one," he laughed. "Papa's getting dizzy."

"She kept saying 'fi, fi' while you were gone, but none of us knew what she wanted," Victoria told him.

"Guess I should have told you before I left, about that little game of fly we play," Diego said.

"How did everything go while we were gone? Did my little Princess give you any trouble while I was away?" Diego asked his mother.

"She was no trouble. Without her two big brothers around teasing her she was a perfect little angel."

"I know better than that. She is my daughter," he laughed as he gave Vicky a hug and she giggled.

"Did the boys behave themselves while you were gone?" Maria asked.

"Surprisingly, they behaved quite well. Aunt Anna told me they were perfect little gentlemen. However, she did say Charlie Joe reminded her of me when you and Papa took us to visit them when we were youngsters."

"And my son, how did you behave?"

"I don't know. You'll have to ask Charlie Joe that question. I'm sure he'll give you a detailed report."

"The boys told me they rode the mares home between San Antonio and here."

"Yes, they did. But, I don't suppose they happened to mention those horses they rode were on very short lead ropes that Robert and I had a firm hand on."

"I believe they did fail to mention that."

"Since we didn't have saddles for them they had to ride bareback. I was surprised and proud to see how well they both rode without benefit of a saddle," Diego told her.

By the time Maria showed Robert to the room where he would be staying and he and Diego got cleaned up, it was time for supper.

"Since we wanted to get the horses here as quickly as possible, we didn't rent a wagon to bring all our things to the ranch. Robert and I thought we would go back to the station in the morning and get them," Diego said, while they were eating.

"I know you're both tired. Why don't you let Cody and me go instead," Antonio offered.

"That sounds like a good idea, but Robert and I need to go to be sure we get everything."

"Diego, you don't need to go. I know you want to check on the ranch and find out how things went while you were gone. I can go to be sure we get it all," Robert offered.

"Thanks. I believe I'll take you up on that."

"I'll take you," Antonio offered. "I know in the morning, Cody will want to check over the horses you brought back with you."

The next morning, after Robert and Antonio left and the boys were outside doing their chores, Maria and Diego were in the library talking and watching Vicky play with her doll.

"It sure is good to be home," Diego told her.

"It's good to have you home. Now do you want to tell me the real reason you bought four horses and why Robert came home with you?"

"I couldn't decide which of the four I wanted, so I bought them all."

"Was it that, or because you saw how monetarily deprived your family in Virginia was?"

"Oh Mama, you wouldn't believe how they live. They've managed to keep the house and all their acreage, but everything is in terrible condition. The war, that hardly affected us, nearly devastated them and all of that part of the country. I just had to do something."

"You don't need to apologize to me for your generosity. I'm proud of what you did to help them. It's just what your father would have done. And Robert?" she asked.

"He had just finished his schooling and there were more people on the plantation than they could comfortably support. Since there are very few jobs in the area for young men, I talked to him about coming here to live and he accepted my offer."

"In other words you told him what a wonderful place it is to live and how we really need a another hand on the ranch."

"Something, like that. But I didn't tell him anything that wasn't the truth. I thought, if he got here and decided he didn't want to be a cowboy, he had a better chance of getting a job in San Antonio than he would have in Richmond or the surrounding area."

"We enjoyed our visit very much. Virginia is a beautiful part of the country and everyone we came in contact with was friendly, but I wouldn't want to live there. Everything is so neat and proper and rather formal. Just the short time we were there, I began to feel closed in. I can just imagine how Papa felt living there. I'm sure glad he came to Texas."

"I am too." Maria said and gave him a loving smile.

"You're another reason I'm glad Papa came to Texas. I can't imagine having one of those prim and proper ladies I met for my mother."

"You don't think I'm prim and proper?" his mother teased.

"I think you know the answer to that question," he laughed.

"Robert, I hardly had a chance to talk to you yesterday before you and Antonio headed back to San Antonio. I hope you will enjoy living here," Maria said the next evening at supper.

"Oh. I know I will. While we were in San Antonio I bought a western style saddle. If I'm going to live here, I want to be a real Texan."

"I'm afraid you're going to have a lot of adjustments to make. If you find being a cowboy isn't what you want to do, please feel free to find something that makes you happy. If you decide you have to leave the ranch, we'll fully understand. More than anything, we want you to be happy."

"Thank you, ma'am. Diego has already told me about some of the new things I'll have to become accustomed to."

"While you were gone I looked at the horses you brought. They are all beautiful."

"Thank you, ma'am. They aren't even some of our best horses. Diego told us he was afraid our best stock wasn't tough enough for Texas."

I wonder if it was that or the fact Diego wanted to buy the horses your family would have the hardest time selling and would get the least for, she wondered.

"Did Diego tell you there's a big race in Kentucky where the best horses in the country race? My family's going to enter one of our stallions in the race next year. If he does well, we'll be able to raise our stud fees and sell our horses at a higher price."

"Yes, he told us a little about it. I hope your horse makes a good showing."

"Thank you, ma'am. I'm sure he will. The only horses in the area who can even come close to outrunning him are those that have some of our horses' blood in them. I sure wish I could be there next May and see the race for myself."

"Maybe that can be arranged," Maria said. She looked at Diego, who discreetly nodded his head in agreement.

"Diego, while you were gone there was something I thought about a lot. I decided I would like for you and the children to move into the house with me. That is, if you want to."

"Are you sure?" he asked.

"Yes. Your father built this house with the intention of it being filled with children and happy people. It will make me very happy to have all of you here.

"A full house will help me not miss your father so much. Since Noelle and Marcus married, the house is too empty and quiet. In fact, it was that way before then. Noelle didn't make enough noise to make this old house the home I'm accustomed to. And, I'm sure, before long Robert will want his own house."

"If it's noise you want, those three children of mine can certainly furnish you with that," Diego laughed.

"The children are already spending more time here than in your house. The four of you might as well move in and call it home. You'll also have more room."

"Thanks, Mama. The house was large enough when it was just the boys and me but they're not happy about having to share a room, since we have Vicky now.

"To be perfectly honest, I've never quite gotten use to living in that house without Vivienne. I'm sure the boys have felt the same."

"Why on earth didn't you tell me that? You could have been living here all along."

"I don't know. I guess I thought we would eventually get use to it. Beside, I didn't want to be an imposition to you."

"The four of you could never be an imposition to me. You know I love being surrounded by family."

"The boys will be thrilled to move in here with you. Just try not to spoil them and Vicky too much."

"If you're going to be living in the house with me, I'll treat them just as I did you and your brothers and sisters when you were growing up."

"Do you really think you can be that tough on them?" He grinned.

"If I'm not, your father will haunt me," she laughed.

THE END